SISTER SPIDER
KNOWS ALL

SISTER SPIDER
KNOWS ALL

Adrian Fogelin

CP
JR

Published by
PEACHTREE PUBLISHERS, LTD.
1700 Chattahoochee Avenue
Atlanta, Georgia 30318-2112

www.peachtree-online.com

Text © 2003 by Adrian Fogelin

Cover design by Loraine M. Joyner
Book design by Melanie M. McMahon

Manufactured in the United States of America
10 9 8 7 6 5 4 3 2 1
First Edition

ISBN 1-56145-290-4

Library of Congress Cataloging-in-Publication Data

Fogelin, Adrian.
Sister Spider Knows All / written by Adrian Fogelin.-- 1st ed.
      p. cm.
Summary: Twelve-year-old Rox and her grandmother Mimi sell at a flea market every weekend to supplement the family's only income, that of construction worker and college student, cousin John Martin.
   ISBN 1-56145-290-4
[1. Flea markets--Fiction. 2. Grandmothers--Fiction. 3. Cousins--Fiction. 4. Poor--Fiction. 5. Family life--Fiction.] I. Title.

PZ7.F72635 So 2003
[Fic]   2003004875

Visit the author's website at
www.adrianfogelin.com

For my daughter, Josie, and her fiancé, Marco,
who came halfway around the world to find her.
Buona fortuna!

Special thanks to my editor, Vicky Holifield,
who always finds the good.

Thanks as always to my buddies, the Wednesday Night Writers.

Table of Contents

Chapter 1
The Show

Don't strain nothin'," Mimi warned, watching me duckwalk a basket of grapes back to the tailgate of the truck. "Remember, Rox, you're a girl."

"Only two more, Mimi," I said, handing the basket down to John Martin.

Mimi and I sell grapes at the flea market this time of year—deep purple muscadines and scuppernongs with pearly skins like big gold bath beads.

I'm not being disrespectful calling my grandmother Mimi. Her Christian name is Marilyn. I made up "Mimi" when I was learning to talk. Calling her that may sound lame, especially for a twelve year old, but it's a little late to change.

"You be careful too, John Martin," she fussed at my cousin, bracing her heavy forearms against the arms of the wheelchair and leaning forward. "Backs are funny things."

"I got it, Ma," he said. To my twenty-three-year-old cousin, Mimi's always been Ma—even though she's really his aunt.

It's complicated. His mother died and Mimi raised him.

My mother disappeared. About all I know is that her name is Helen. If I ask questions about her, Mimi always says, Tell you sometime. Sometime when? I ask. I'll let you know, she answers.

Mimi says our family may not be a greeting card, but the three of us together—John Martin, her, and me—are family enough for anyone.

"I swear," Mimi grumped as I swung the last basket of grapes into my cousin's arms, "between the picking and lifting, grapes are too danged much work."

My cousin winked at me. "We do the picking and lifting," he whispered. "All she does is complain."

"Complaining's her job," I whispered back.

"And she sure is good at it."

I nudged a bucket of zinnias toward the tailgate with the toe of my sneaker. Water sloshed. The legs of my overalls were already soaked. John Martin and I had cut the flowers before the sun came up and burned the dew off. A pretty nice job if you don't mind getting up at five.

The last thing John Martin unloaded was me—which was probably more hazardous for his back than moving a whole truckload of grapes. He grabbed me by the waist and hefted me off the tailgate. "You study today," he said as he plopped me down. "Don't tell me you forgot. I put your books over there."

"Okay, okay," I said, as the huge hand on the back of my neck swiveled my head toward the books piled under our table. "I see. I'll get around to it." The hand squeezed my neck. "Ow, that hurts," I said. Even though it didn't.

"Cut it out, you big old bear," Mimi scolded. "You don't know your own strength."

John Martin pushed the bill of his baseball cap up with his thumb, so I could see his eyes. "I mean it now, Rox. Don't rile the big old bear. Do your homework." He tugged the hat down again, ambled over to the truck, and climbed in.

I was walking toward our table under the roof of the open shed when he tapped the horn. "Start before the crowd gets here, okay?" And he turned on the ignition.

Leaving a blue cloud, John Martin headed for his construction job, his textbooks wedged behind the seat. He studies on his lunch break and any other chance he gets. Ever since Grandpa Bill died he's had to work to help Mimi cover the bills. Taking two courses a semester at Tallahassee Community College, he won't set any records, but he'll make it. He's what teachers call an achiever.

Not me. I hate school. I'm no good at it, except for maybe English. Luckily, it would be hours and hours before the truck came back to fetch us, plenty of time to do homework later.

I took a scuppernong off the top of one of the baskets and bit down. *Pop* went the thick skin, and the rest of the grape jetted into my mouth.

"And grapes are too much work to eat," Mimi commented, as she dug for cigarettes in her big black purse. "Especially with dentures."

Grabbing one of the poles that held up the roof, I swung way out and spit the seeds a good six feet. "Well, I like them." I wiped my mouth with the back of my hand. "My mom liked them too, didn't she?"

Click, Mimi flipped the top of her lighter, lit a Marlboro, and took a deep drag. Her words came out with smoke signals. "Tell you sometime."

"When sometime?"

"I'll let you know." And then she changed the subject. "What's the magic number today?"

I took a quick look at my hand. "Eighty-seven eleven," I said, reading the number I'd written there. That was how much we needed to pay the electric bill due Tuesday. Property taxes were coming up soon, plus insurance for the truck, but I'd mark those numbers on my hand on other days.

"Eight-seven-one-one," said Mimi. "Let's get to work."

I took a folded sheet off the top of one of the baskets. As I shook it out, the wind caught it. I felt like it might lift me right off the concrete slab and sail me up and up...over the tin roofs, over the vendors' pickups and vans.

Mimi slapped the sheet down on the plywood table and held it until I set a basket of grapes on each end. She reached out and ran a

3

hand over the bright yarns of my sweater. The soft, old skin of her face crumpled in a smile. "Glad you like the sweater, Rox."

I slung an arm around her neck. "I like it big time." She had crocheted my sweater using leftover yarns from the afghans she sells. Like the afghans, it was made of stitched-together granny squares—a blanket with sleeves.

Across the center aisle and two booths down, tiny Mrs. Yu was unloading inventory from the trunk of her ancient Cadillac. "Your cheatin' heart, will tell on you..." she sang along with the radio.

I waved. "Morning, Mrs. Yu."

"Good morning, Rox." She lifted a lacy party dress to the overhead rack with a hook. Stiff and starchy with layer upon layer of petticoats, the dresses she sells would scratch the life out of you if you had to wear one. But walk under the rack and look up, and the dresses bloom like flowers.

Mimi took one last drag on her cigarette. "Time to tour the Show." The Show is what she calls the flea market. A big part of her workday is spent buzzing around in her chair, catching up on the latest gossip. She dropped and crushed the butt, then tried to start the wheelchair. But it sat there, dead. "Piece of junk!" she muttered, fiddling with the controls. She bought the chair from Micky Green, a few booths down. John Martin pitched a fit when he came to pick us up that day and found her sitting in it. He said even though it was hard for her to walk, she shouldn't give up. She told him she hoped he had arthritis when he got old so he'd appreciate all she suffered.

I don't mind the wheelchair. Without it she'd sit at the booth all day. With it she can go—at least when the chair works.

"Shoot, shoot, shoot!" she yelled, smacking the controls.

"Need help with that, Miss Marilyn?" Danny, our neighbor across the aisle, hitched up his jeans and strolled over. He fiddled a little with the wheelchair too. "There you go," he said as the motor buzzed. And with a lurch, Mimi was off.

I began heaping grapes in individual baskets, putting a few extra-pretty ones on top to make a customer stop—and reach for a wallet.

The junk came next. During the week people drop it by the house. We sell what we can and take half of whatever we can get. They think because it's a flea market folks will buy anything.

And they will, but only if you arrange the stuff so it looks pretty, not junky. In two years of selling I've learned that everything is valuable in some way. Finding the good and featuring it is my specialty. I don't hide the bad parts—that would be cheating—but I don't point them out. I let the bad parts speak for themselves.

Sometimes finding the good is hard. That's because there is junk and there is Junk. Most of what I had to work with today was little-*j* junk, like a collection of empty perfume bottles, McDonald's Happy Meal prizes, a box of costume jewelry, half a dozen vintage Barbies. "Vintage" means the dolls have ratty hair and their shoes are missing. Some vendors would give up and dump the whole mess in a heap and let the customers paw through it. Not me. Since their shoes were missing, I posed the Barbies in a beach scene. Hamburglar and Grimace joined them on a washcloth beach towel.

I unpacked cartons of cookware and kitchen accessories, T-shirts and cowboy boots, general bric-a-brac, and the world's ugliest beer stein. I arranged them, then walked around the front of the table to check the effect.

"Lookin' good, Rox! Wanna see what you can do with used tires?" Danny dropped a couple of tires off the back of his truck. Danny's not a big guy, like John Martin, but he is *seriously* built, and knows it. He wears T-shirts with the sleeves torn off. Women stop all the time, pretending they want tires. "Tires my foot," says Mimi. "They want his body."

"Got donuts in the cab," Danny said as he manhandled a couple of Uniroyals. "Go ahead, Rox. Help yourself."

Danny Swain, The Tire King, said the black letters on the truck door. It opened without a sound on oiled hinges to reveal a Krispy Kreme box on the driver's seat. When I lifted the lid, a dozen glazed donuts gleamed up at me. I picked the best one and held it close to my nose, but all I could smell was rubber.

Smell-wise it would be better if we set up near the jewelry people or the incense sellers, but I like being close to Danny. He tries to help me figure out math. He fixes Mimi's chair. He always brings donuts. And those are just *some* of the good things about Danny Swain. Finding the good applies to people too.

A truck rattled up. The Gonzalez boys, Juan and Marco, were asleep in back, wrapped in blankets and curled around baskets and cartons of fruits and vegetables.

Mr. Gonzalez backed the truck until his tires bucked the edge of the concrete slab. The jolt woke Juan up. He stood, his quilt around him.

"Hey, Superman!" I shouted.

"Hey, Rox-in-socks!" He smiled sleepily, yawned, then poked his brother with his toes. A second mop of shiny black hair popped up.

Mr. Gonzalez climbed down from the truck cab. Stiff after the long drive up from Lake Okeechobee, he strutted in his tall-heeled cowboy boots like a banty rooster. When he reached the back of the pickup and spread his arms, Marco jumped.

"Hey, amigos," Danny yelled, "donuts!" Marco leaped out of his father's arms and raced his brother to Danny's truck.

Mrs. Gonzalez rolled out of the truck cab last, her bright print skirt billowing. Mrs. Gonzalez is fat, but nice-fat, like a stuffed chair. In her arms was the newest Gonzalez, Rosa—just a nub of black hair sticking out of a blanket. Rosa is the same age I was when my mother left. Three months. Mrs. Gonzalez never sets Rosa down.

≈

I Magic-Markered my signs. The one for the empty perfume bottles said Collectibles. Like "vintage," it's a fancy word for junk. I sat on my stool and ate my donut while I waited for customers. My feet rested on the stack of schoolbooks. I purposely didn't look at them. It wasn't like the kids in my class were studying. They were probably still lazing around in their pajamas. What's the big deal about school, anyway? The only reason to go is to get a job, and I already have one.

Too bad John Martin disagrees. According to him, school is my real job. He says in the long run school is the only thing that gets a person up off the bottom.

Mimi insists that we're miles above the bottom; you're at the bottom when you live in a cardboard box. We own twenty-two acres and a house free and clear.

But if we *are* up off the bottom—and I'm not one hundred percent sure we are—it's because of the money we make on weekends. Mimi couldn't do the flea market without me. She would never get here. I bring her coffee, which she drinks before opening her eyes. Two cups later she groans, then dresses. I redo her buttons and hand her lipstick. By then she's alive enough to fix her hair, which I spray until it's crunchy and weather-resistant. "I don't know why I even bother with the Show," she complains as I stuff her feet in her shoes.

But I know why. She bothers because we need the money. And she bothers because, since we quit going to church, every friend she has in the world runs a booth at the Tallahassee flea market.

I have friends here too. Lots of friends. And it's never boring. Sooner or later you see everything at the Show. *Everything.* It's the world's best parade.

~

"Cock-a-poos," said Mimi, smacking into the leg of the table with one wheel. "Right next to Marie. Cutest little things you ever seen." She was back from her round of visits. In her lap were two jumbo cans of stew, and a smaller one with no label from the mystery bin at the Dent & Ding booth. "Go on, Rox," she urged, stashing the cans under our table. "Take a puppy break. I'll watch things here."

"I don't know… There are lots of shoppers." While she was away I had sold four baskets of grapes plus a perfume bottle shaped like a treasure chest. "All right, but I'll be right back," I told her. "Don't go anywhere, okay?"

"Pups-of-the-week!" I shouted, swooping in on Charles's booth. I plunged a hand into a jar of Libertys. The red, white, and blue marbles squirmed away from my fingers. Even in the hottest weather the marbles in the jars on Charles's stand are slippery-cool, like fish. Today they were icy. I pulled my hand out and skipped backwards a couple of steps. "Ya coming?"

"Can't. My dad'd kill me." He topped off a jar of yellow and green John Deeres, then flicked his hair out of his eyes. Charles has the strangest haircut, long in the front, short everywhere else.

"Come *on*, Charles, you know you want to!" Charles is thirteen, but he's in seventh too. He stayed back. He's quitting school when he turns fourteen, then he'll have his own stand. He says at fourteen it's legal to drop out. If I thought I'd live to see fifteen, I'd quit at fourteen too. But I wouldn't. John Martin would see to that. "Well, I'm going."

"Hold up." He leaned over the counter and looked as far as he could down the long row of tables. "You see him?" he asked. When I shook my head, he dug the wad of bills out of the cash box and shoved it in his pocket. "Let's go."

Hoping Charles wouldn't notice, I slowed down so he could keep up. His right foot turns in like it's on the wrong leg. His right hand is funny too, small and shriveled. He looks better behind the table. Sometimes, surrounded by all those shiny marbles, he looks almost handsome, in a Charles kind of way.

Too bad his mom cuts his hair.

"You working on Edison yet?" he asked, pushing his hair back out of his eyes.

"Trying to," I said. "But my cousin's too busy to drive me to the library and my grandma won't make him. We have this old encyclopedia that has a whopping page and a half about Edison in it. She says I should write the report out of that."

"Could I borrow it sometime?" I guess he was having trouble getting his hands on five sources too. Flunking stuff wasn't always our fault.

~

I never said I was their daughter. I just stood close to the couple that was cooing at the fuzzy, wriggling pile of puppies and whined, "Can I hold one, please?" The woman with the pups-of-the-week called me "Sugar," then frowned when the couple walked away. Too late. By then I had a puppy in my arms.

"Oh, Bobby," I said to Charles. "Mom'll just love this one."

"She might even want two," he said, playing along. "One for me and one for you, Cindy." The woman went back to smiling.

Mimi's friend, Spice Marie, who was selling a bottle of onion flakes at the next booth, looked like she was going to bust if she didn't laugh out loud. Spice Marie is a regular, like us. She knew we weren't Bobby and Cindy. She also knew there wasn't a chance in the world of either one of us taking a pup home.

Charles buried his face in puppy fur. He'd die if someone from school saw him do that, but he knew I wouldn't get on him about it.

"Hey, Bobby," I joked, as we walked back. "What's up with you and those pants?" Shiny and black, they hung low on his butt. "I can see your drawers."

"You're *supposed* to," said Charles, faking a strut. "I'm stylin'."

One good tug would bring his stylin' pants down. With anyone else I might've done it, but for Charles, being cool is thin as a coat of paint. Why wreck it?

A skinny man waved at us. "Hey, Rox. Hey, Charles!" He was surrounded by china cats, dragons, and Buddhas, all belching smoke.

"Hey, Mr. Finch," we said together.

The incense seller pulled out a bandanna and blew his nose. The rims of his eyes were pink. Mr. Finch is his own worst advertisement. Mimi's always telling him he should retire. "Tried that once," he says. "Couldn't afford it." He says the Show helps him buy the little extras, like food and medicine. "By the way," he called after us. "Your old man's looking for you, Charles."

"Uh-oh," said Charles. "I'm in a world of hurt now." He made it sound like a joke, but he hitched up his pants and stumbled back as fast as he could. His dad was at their display, waiting for him.

"I was only gone a mi…minute…" Charles stuttered, pulling his head down like he was trying to disappear into himself. Even though it was kind of my fault he was in trouble, I slipped away into the crowd. Charles would be humiliated if I stuck around, and he'd still catch it from his dad.

Mimi was parked under Mrs. Yu's dress display, chatting. "I been watching our things from here," she called.

Everything was exactly where it had been when I went on puppy break. Mimi hadn't sold a single grape. I stared at the number printed on my hand. Eight-seven-one-one. I slapped on my selling smile and went to work.

Chapter 2
Spitting Lessons

W here the heck is he?" Mimi said. Her red lipstick had spi-
dered up into the little wrinkles around her mouth. Her
hair, all poofy and sprayed and seemingly indestructible
when we left the house, had blown flat. All the other vendors had
gone home. "Hope him and that truck aren't rolled over in a ditch
somewheres."

My shadow stretched long across the concrete floor. I stared at the
dusty toes of my sneaks and tried not to imagine John Martin's truck
rolled over in a ditch. I wiped my hands on the legs of my overalls.
After handling grapes and junk all day they felt icky. I folded my
sweater and draped it carefully over an empty basket.

Mimi shook the last cigarette out of the pack. "That boy is never
late." She had smoked the cigarette down to the filter before the
truck clattered up.

"What the—" Mimi stared. On top of being late, John Martin
had someone with him. A girl scrambled out right behind my cousin
and stood next to him, grinning.

My cousin scuffed the ground with a work boot. "This is my
study partner from calculus class," he said. "Her name is Lucy."

The girl grabbed John Martin by the back pocket of his jeans and
hung on. "Everhart," she added. "Lucy Everhart."

Lucy Everhart was skinny and pale with white-blond hair. What
little there was of her chewed-off nails was painted purple. Add a

couple of eyebrows and you could almost call her pretty. But her clothes were beautiful, especially her yellow sweater, which looked as soft as the angora rabbits Ferry Morgan sells in the next wing of the flea market.

I stuffed my granny square sweater down into the empty basket, then checked quick to see if Mimi had noticed. But she couldn't seem to take her eyes off the hand that was latched onto our John Martin. I thought for sure she was going to slap it. "Why is she here?"

Lucy Everhart twisted the edge of the pocket, then lifted her chin. "I'm his girlfriend."

John Martin flinched.

"Girlfriend!" Mimi sputtered. "Well, I never..." She rolled the chair over to the truck, grabbed the door handle, and pulled herself up. She wrenched the door open and flopped back onto the seat. "You been running the AC?" she shouted. John Martin never ran it for us, even if we begged. He said it wrecked his gas mileage. But he had run it for Lucy Everhart.

"Better pack up," he mumbled. I tossed empty baskets in the back of the truck. He muscled the wheelchair up over the tailgate. Danny usually helps him with it but the Tire King was long gone. Lucy Everhart tried to help but we have a routine, John Martin and me.

When we were all packed, I climbed in back. Lucy Everhart went around to get in the cab, but Mimi wouldn't surrender an inch of seat. Next thing I knew, Lucy was stepping up on the bumper and over the tailgate.

"I've never ridden in the back of a pickup before," she whooped as we bounced over the hummocky ground behind the flea market. Where has she been all her life? I wondered. When we hit paved road and the wind picked up, she spread her arms and yipped like a coyote.

"How long have you two been boyfriend and girlfriend?" I yelled.

Lucy checked her watch. "Fourteen minutes?"

~

I helped Mimi out of the front seat. "Keep your eyes in your head," she told Lucy Everhart. "At least it's not a mobile home. And mind you don't trip over one of my children," she warned, pointing out the gaggle of garden sculptures that were scattered around the weed patch we call a lawn.

"Welcome to Ma's roadside attraction," said my cousin. I had never noticed how many lawn statues we'd traded for at the Show: mushrooms and rhinos, saints and gnomes. What was Lucy thinking as she wandered among them? Most were no taller than her boots, but a few, like the rhino and the pig, came up to her thighs. Lucy straddled the pig and sat, gawking at the house.

I looked too, and saw what she saw: shutters that hung like droopy eyelids, the sagging porch. Our house had settled, like a sleeping dog.

"Maybe she'll just stay in the yard, riding that pig," Mimi whispered as I helped her climb the stairs onto the porch. But Lucy swung her leg back over and trotted up the steps ahead of us.

"Let me help you with that door, Mrs. Piermont."

Mimi gave the keys to me, but Lucy looked so eager to help I handed them to her. Lucy unlocked and let herself in.

"Well, make yourself at home, why don't you?" Mimi puffed, still trying to catch her breath.

All was silent for a moment, then, from inside the house, we heard a startled yelp.

Mimi smiled. "Sounds like she met Milton."

When the rest of us went in, we found Lucy pinned to the wall, one big paw on each shoulder. Her head was turned, but with his super-long tongue, Milton wasn't having any trouble licking her eyeballs.

"What kind of dog are you?" Lucy asked, trying to push him away.

"Milton's half dog, half cow," I said.

John Martin threw an arm around our dog's chest and pried him off Lucy Everhart. He lifted a hand to brush dog hairs off the front of her sweater—then shoved the hand in his pocket instead.

"Nice to meet you, Milt," Lucy said. She scratched him behind an ear and took a look around. "What a cozy place."

John Martin stared at his boots. Mimi's recliner floated like a raft in front of the TV, a full ashtray balanced on the arm. The rug was scattered with autumn leaves I'd sprayed shiny. They were dry; I just hadn't picked them up yet.

Next, Lucy turned toward the dining room where the table was buried under drifts of Indian corn, wire, paint, bottles of glitter, and bowls of sequins. "The ladies are making inventory," my cousin explained, the tips of his ears turning red.

Lucy Everhart stood, her brand new leather boots on our linty, glittery rug. Suddenly, the sprayed leaves looked cheesy. Everything looked cheesy.

"So," Mimi sighed. "I guess she'll be staying for supper?"

Lucy looked over at John Martin and grinned, showing off blue braces. "That would be super, Mrs. Piermont! Thanks for inviting me."

Mimi heaved another sigh. "Go. Pick grapes for tomorrow. All of you. Shoo!"

John Martin headed straight through the kitchen and out the back door. Milton and I went too. Of course, Lucy followed. It was like there was a magnet inside John Martin dragging her along.

"Wow!" she yelled as we stepped out the back door and under the grape arbor. "I feel like I'm in France!"

John Martin stopped short. "You've been to France?" When she nodded, his shoulders sagged. It seemed like dating someone who had been to France was more than he could handle.

"It's nice here too," I said. "As nice as France." The air smelled sweet, and a little vinegary from the rotting fruit that raccoons and possums had dropped on the ground. They could afford to waste a few; even in France the grapes couldn't hang any thicker. "Grandpa Bill built this arbor himself," I told Lucy, giving one of the posts a slap so she'd notice what a good arbor it was. "He died a couple years ago. Suddenly." I lowered my voice. "Mimi and I are pretty sure he hid a jar of money someplace, only he didn't have time to tell us where."

"You don't even have a clue?" she whispered. "Want me to help you look? I'm good at finding things."

John Martin set a basket on the ground and straightened up. "Cut it out, Rox. There isn't any hidden money." I wanted to punch him. "You're looking at everything Pop left," he said, spreading his arms. "The house, plus twenty-two acres of sand and pines. Pop worked with his back and his hands, not his head. Worked himself to death for next to nothing."

"This is *not* nothing!" I said. "It's beautiful and it's ours!"

"Sure it's pretty, but pretty don't pay the bills. We have to be practical, get our educations."

"And what about this?" I held up my hand and showed him the smeared eighty-seven eleven.

"What is it?" he asked.

How practical can he be when he doesn't even know about the light bill? "Better pick grapes so we have something to sell tomorrow," I said, turning away.

"These don't look like any grapes I've ever seen," Lucy said.

"They're scuppernongs," I told her.

She reached for one. "I've never picked grapes before."

I bugged my eyes. "Never?"

"She don't have to," John Martin said, picking fast. "Her daddy's a doctor."

I picked slowly, as the patches of sky between the leaves turned dusty. I loved this time of day. Just after the sun goes down it seems as if the light comes from *inside* of things. I wanted my cousin to notice that the grapes we picked were glowing. But he was talking about some physics class he planned to take next semester.

Lucy interrupted him. "I've never eaten a scuppernong. Can I try one?"

"Sure," I said. "Put it halfway in your mouth and bite down. The inside of the grape will shoot right out of the skin. After that, just spit out the seeds. Go ahead, John Martin. Show her how. He's the best," I bragged.

My cousin didn't know whether to be embarrassed or proud. He did one grape, tipping his head way back to launch the seeds. "Undisputed champ!" I yelled as his shot splatted against a washtub ten feet away.

After that, John Martin did most of the picking. Lucy and I were trying to hit the tub too, but we couldn't get the right combination of accuracy and distance. Lucy about fainted trying. I guess her daddy the doctor didn't let her spit at home.

~

John Martin backed the truck around the side of the house, weaving between Mimi's sculptures like a barrel racer. Maybe he was showing off for Lucy because he did it kind of fast. He didn't nick a single mushroom or troll—but he ran smack over a bushel basket of grapes.

Splat!

Grapes squirted out of their skins, pelting Lucy and me with grape eyes. Milton took off in a cloud of hair. Lucy fell on the ground laughing. I doubled over hugging my stomach.

John Martin stayed in the truck.

"Gawd!" Lucy threw her legs and arms out straight. "I can hardly breathe."

The truck door whined when it opened, and we laughed even harder.

"I don't see what's so funny." John Martin leaned out the open door. "We're only gonna have to pick us another basket."

Lucy tore up a handful of grass and tossed it like confetti. "Lighten up, Johnny."

Johnny? Nobody called my cousin Johnny. He hated it.

But he didn't correct her. Instead he jumped down from the cab and held his hands out. "Up you go." As he pulled her to her feet, I heard her breath catch. Suddenly, she was standing smack against him. Blue jean to blue jean, yellow sweater to Nascar T-shirt. She craned her neck to look up at him. He looked down. They gazed into each other's eyes.

"Bet supper's ready," I said loudly.

$\sim$

When Grandpa Bill was alive, Mimi used to cook. I mean, *really* cook—pot roast, biscuits, gravy—the works. These days she could barely manage to turn on a burner and stir, but when we came back in the house I could see that she had really knocked herself out. She had cleared the mess off the dining room table. The stew came out of Dent & Ding cans, but she had added dumplings and put out china instead of the usual paper plates. There was even a bowl of olives—probably from the mystery can.

When Lucy excused herself to go to the bathroom, I cut my eyes over toward Mimi.

"I didn't want her to think we were trash," she whispered. "I'm so bushed I could keel over dead," she added for John Martin's benefit.

"This really looks good," Lucy bubbled as she walked back to the table. "We never have dumplings at home."

Mimi looked at her as if she had just announced that she'd never had a glass of water.

"My mother tries to limit starches," Lucy explained. "But I love dumplings! Are they hard to make?"

Mimi sagged, her arms on the table. "Well, they aren't the easiest things in the world."

John Martin nudged my knee with his. These days, Mimi makes her dumplings out of a box. All she does is add milk and stir.

"Could you teach me how to make them sometime?" Lucy begged.

"We'll see." But Mimi looked pleased when Lucy helped herself to another one.

Since Lucy was piling up dumplings, I snagged three more for myself.

John Martin glared.

I froze, a hunk of dumpling halfway to my mouth.

Lucy looked from him to me, then whipped around to face my cousin. "Johnny, don't make her feel bad about her weight. You could damage her for life!" She shook a finger at him. "If you don't watch out you'll make her hate her body!"

John Martin looked distressed. "I wasn't on her about her weight. Hogging three dumplings is bad manners. Damage her for life? Give me a break. You're not a psychologist yet. You haven't taken the first class." He sopped stew up with a dumpling and mumbled, "Bet you got that 'hate her body' thing offa Oprah."

Lucy's fork clattered to her plate. "There is nothing wrong with Oprah!" And Mimi nodded; it was the first thing they'd agreed on since Lucy climbed out of my cousin's truck.

While Lucy and Mimi had their moment of Oprah-agreement, I stared at the dumplings. It's not like I'm huge-fat or anything, just stocky. Sometimes at school, where the popular girls are skinny little twigs, I feel like an elephant in overalls. But even if I sewed my lips shut and quit eating altogether, I'd never be one of them because I'm tall and big boned like John Martin.

After Lucy's comments the dumplings looked gluey and hard to swallow. I ate one and left the rest for Milton.

"See that, Johnny?" said Lucy. "She's starving herself already."

~

I woke to rain pinging on the tin roof. It *had* to stop by morning. Wet weather is bad for the Show. Rain means fewer customers. Folks who think it'd be fun to rent a table for a day and sell junk out of their garages stay in bed. Regulars like us, who wouldn't miss a day for the Second Coming, set up our booths, lean on our elbows, and stare down the empty aisles.

As the rain fell harder, I thought about the math take-home test in my backpack. Rain meant more time to work on it, not that that would help.

According to Mimi, the girls in our family aren't the brightest bulbs on the tree. By that she meant me and her, but I wondered if that included my mother. I kind of think it did because one day, when I was looking through some old magazines, I found a spelling list with her name at the top. It was the first thing of hers I had ever found. I looked at it so often I memorized the words: ballerina, diorama, edible, ferret, hideous, justify, loquacious, persuasive, quagmire, and yodel. She had had to write sentences using the words.

The loquacious ballarina yodeled in the hideous quagmire.

Can the persuasive feret justify his edible diorama?

You don't have to be a brainiac to spell, but making them into sentences, she had misspelled two of the words. Someone with a red pen had circled the misspellings and then written: *One sentence for each word, please!*

I still have the list, along with a few other things I've found over the years, like a pink plastic barrette from the back of a drawer, a hairbrush from under the mattress. I keep all her stuff in a shoe box in my closet, but it's a puzzle with most of the pieces missing.

When I was little I believed in Santa and the tooth fairy, so when Mimi said my mother had vanished, *poof,* like a genie going into a bottle, I believed her.

As I grew older I realized that the story of my mother wasn't a fairy tale, that she had gone somewhere in the real world. For a while I bugged everyone: Mimi, Grandpa Bill, John Martin; I bugged John Martin most. The adults wouldn't tell me anything, but he was in high school so he wasn't a *real* adult. He didn't want to talk either.

"Tell me one thing about her," I begged. "Just *one* thing."

"She had long wavy brown hair."

Before he could clam up I asked him to describe her eyes, *pleeeaaase*…and promised to leave him alone after that. When he said green, I pushed him. "What kind of green? Yellow-green or blue-green?"

"Sneaky green," he said. "Like a cat's. Why do you want to know about her anyway? She deserted us, Rox." And that told me the most. Definitely no magical *poof.* She had left because she wanted to.

I thought about it a lot for a while. Now, as the rain pelted the roof, I wondered again, why had she left? The reason that seemed worst—and truest—was that she had left because she didn't love me. Even though I had thought the same thing plenty of times before, my mother not loving me still gave me an empty, achy feeling. So I slid away from the reasons why she had left and concentrated on *how.*

How had she gotten away from here? We're in the middle of nowhere. No buses. No trains. Maybe Helen had run down the path to a waiting car. Maybe my father was driving. I've asked Mimi about him too, but if my mother is a "tell you sometime," my father has been erased so hard he is nothing but a hole in the paper.

Lying in my mother's old bed, listening to the rain, I realized I was in no big hurry to find out about her. Mimi's "tell you sometime" was good enough for now.

Chapter 3
Selling the *Titanic*

Mimi sat hunched in her wheelchair, playing solitaire, an afghan around her shoulders. A slow, steady drizzle had been falling all morning, like someone who was worn out with crying but couldn't quite stop. Blue plastic tarps snapped in the wind. The roof over our table had sprung a leak. The rain dripped into a cup. *Plonk...plonk...plonk.* Mimi's hand darted out from under the afghan. She fingered one of the cards that lay facedown on the edge of our table.

"No peeking, Mimi!" I scolded.

She bent a corner of the card up, ignoring me and the few customers who were straggling through. I tried to pitch them, but they seemed too depressed to buy. After saying hi to half a dozen people who didn't answer, I opened my math book.

I was struggling with problem four when a voice asked, "What're you doing?"

I barely glanced at Marco, who had wandered over from the Gonzalez vegetable stand. "Dividing fractions," I said. I erased my answer, leaving another smudge.

He hung his arm around my waist and pressed his cheek into my side. "What's a fraction, Rox-in-socks?"

"A fraction is like, if I cut a pie in pieces. Say I cut the pie in half and I keep one half and give the other half to you." I wrote 1/2 on the piece of paper. "See, the one is the pie, and the two is the number of pieces. One for you and one for me. Understand?"

Marco thought about it, then looked up at me, all serious. "What kind of pie?"

"Doesn't matter, you doof. And I'm supposed to have quiet. This is a test."

But he hung onto my sweater. "Play hide with me, Rox-in-socks, come on."

"Can't. I have twenty more problems."

He tugged at my sweater, stretching it. "Close your eyes. Count to fifty."

"I told you, no..." I looked at the next problem. *Twenty-seven sixty-fourths?* They had to be kidding.

"Just thirty," Marco begged. "Count to thirty, okay?"

"Oh, all right." I closed my eyes. "One, two, three... Hey, Marco, stay between the velvet paintings and the silk flowers, okay?"

"Yeah, okay."

Listening to his voice, I could tell which way he was going. I counted slowly to thirty, then yelled, "Ready or not, here I come," and headed in that direction.

"Hey-hey, Rox." Jerome sat on a stool, smoking a cigar, surrounded by velvet Elvises, snorting bulls, and jaguars crouched in trees. Jerome is Jamaican, with thick, knotty dreads and bulgy eyes. Scary looking. Sometimes I think he intimidates customers into buying just by looking at them. They don't know that Jerome is a marshmallow.

"Slow day," I said, studying the sad expression on the nearest Elvis.

"Like watching paint dry." Jerome blew a lazy smoke ring. As I caught it on my finger, the tip of Jerome's tongue darted out and another one wobbled my way. I looked for Marco behind a leaned-up picture. "Not even warm," Jerome said.

"No hints," said a small voice.

I turned quick. Where had it come from? All the vendors were smiling; for some, it was the first smile of the day. They knew where he was.

"Cold," they called as I checked under the tablecloth on Miss Louise's table.

"Freezing! Arctic!" they shouted when I crouched and looked under the row of pickups parked behind the sheds.

I wove between plastic-stone fountains, looking. "Wrong galaxy," said Jerome, then he chugged out a chain of smoke rings.

At this rate, I'd never get back to dividing fractions.

Then I noticed Danny the Tire King, who was sitting on the dropped tailgate of his truck. He was eating a chili dog from the concession, but his eyes kept wandering to the stacks of tires.

"I wonder where that kid could be?" I said. I cocked my head toward the piled tires and shrugged at Danny.

Danny swung his legs and grinned. He knew I knew.

I wandered through the stacks of tires, peering into each one. "I'm sure a boy couldn't get down into these tires," I said loudly. I heard a giggle, and for a moment shiny black hair showed above the top of a pile near the back. I reached over and tapped Marco on the head. "Busted!" I said.

Marco turned his face up. "Scratch my nose, okay? I can't reach."

"Scratch your own nose, hombre." Danny left the hotdog on the tailgate and lifted the top two tires. He hauled Marco out.

I headed back to my fractions, but Marco buzzed me, taking quick jabs with his fists. "You gotta hide too! At least one time, you gotta hide! That's the deal."

"I have twenty problems to go."

"One teeny-eeny time," he begged. Then he just closed his eyes and started to count fast. "One, two, three..."

I ran. "Would you slow down!" I hid in the easiest place I could find: under the cloth on Miss Louise's table.

At first I heard him, sometimes close, sometimes far away. "Am I getting warm? Am I warm?"

"You got icicles on your skinny butt, man," Jerome answered.

After a while, I didn't hear Marco's voice anymore. To pass the time I started retying Miss Louise's pink sneakers. As large as she is, it's hard for her to see—let alone reach—her shoes. I was pulling her laces tight when something poked me in the rear. I whipped around. The toes of a pair of blue and white Nikes showed below the edge of the tablecloth.

"Tupelo is a kind of gum tree," said Miss Louise, beginning her pitch. "Its flowers make the very best honey in the world."

The Nikes shifted. "Can we pa-leeze go now, Mom? I promised Joelle I'd call."

"I'm sure Joelle won't die waiting another half hour, Sara."

I quit breathing. The shoes and the whiny voice belonged to Sara Michaels, the second most popular girl in my class. If she found out I was under the table and spread it around, I'd have to go somewhere else and start a new life.

"Would you like to buy a jar today?" Miss Louise asked brightly.

"Mo-om." The heels of the Nikes bounced impatiently.

"I'll think about it," said Mrs. Michaels, and the Nikes walked away.

"What's there to think about?" Miss Louise grumbled. Her chair creaked as she leaned down to lift the edge of the cloth. "Might as well come out, Rox. Marco's bagging zucchini at his folks' stand."

I put a finger on my lips and shook my head. "Is she gone?" I whispered.

Miss Louise narrowed her eyes. "You mean, Miss Whiny-Hiney?" she whispered back. "Not hardly. Jerome is trying to sell her mom a painting. Fat lotta good it'll do him. I'll let you know when the coast is clear." The tablecloth dropped. I had just finished retying her shoes when it lifted again. "She's down by Charms 'n' Chains checking out birthstone pendants."

I tugged at the cloth. "Not far enough."

She tugged back. "Maybe not, but if you don't get out from under there you'll miss a sale. Your grandma has a live one who she is flat ignoring."

I stuck my head up like a prairie dog and peered over the table. I could see Sara, and I could see the live one, a woman who was lingering over the collectible perfume bottles. She held one shaped like a ship in her hand. In a second she would put it down and walk away. Mimi, who was beating herself at solitaire, wasn't doing a thing to close the sale.

So Sara wouldn't spot me, I slipped back to our table from behind and said the first thing I could think of to the customer. "That bottle is a genuine replica of the *Titanic,* before it hit the iceberg."

"The *Titanic?*" The woman's eyes got all dreamy. I felt sort of guilty, but it *could* have been the *Titanic.*

Sara gazed back my way, but she was eyeing Danny and his superior muscles. Sick, I thought. He's old enough to be your daddy.

My customer held the bottle up in the weak, rainy light trying to see its color. She sighed. "Didn't you just *love* the movie?"

"Amethyst," I said as Sara turned away again. "It's one of the rarer colors." I hadn't seen the movie and I wasn't going to lie about it.

I could tell Sara was trying to talk her mother into buying her something. She stamped a foot like a two year old.

"I certainly don't need an empty bottle," said the woman, but she didn't set it down.

Sara huffed away from her mother and disappeared in the crowd.

"I already have so much useless junk..." The woman hesitated, the hand holding the bottle halfway to the table. It was the hesitation of someone teetering on the edge of buying another piece of useless junk.

I took the bottle out of her hand. "Here, let me wrap it for you." I put newspaper around it carefully, like it was special, and snapped open a bag. I handed over her purchase and made change.

Mimi cocked her head toward the woman with the *Titanic* bottle, who was about to be trapped among the velvet paintings by an evil look from Jerome. "You're good, Rox. You could sell a saddle to a horse."

~

The sun broke through in the last hour. The parking lot steamed, and suddenly it was hot, but without the rain, things picked up. "Feeding frenzy," declared Mimi, sweeping her solitaire game into the open mouth of her purse and turning on the charm.

We sold eight baskets of grapes, four more bottles, and a washboard with "Fels Naphtha Soap" painted on the wooden part. We'd been hauling that board back and forth for months. I stuffed bills in one pocket, coins in the other. Between the crunch of the bills and the coins pulling my pocket down, I felt rich.

At the last minute, I almost sold the ugly Oktoberfest beer stein—which was turning out to be harder than selling a saddle to a horse. Packing up, Mimi held the stein out over the concrete floor. "How about it, Rox? Should I put us out of its misery?"

"Nah. We'd only have to sweep it up."

So she wrapped it in paper one more time and stuck it in the box.

We were usually still packing when John Martin rolled up, but everything, including the sheet off the plywood table, had been boxed. "I hope he don't plan to make this a habit," said Mimi. We had the place all to ourselves again.

~

"You get your homework done?"

I swear those were the first words out of my cousin's mouth when he drove up.

Mimi was not one bit distracted by the homework question. Lucy Everhart was hanging off John Martin again. She held his right hand in both of hers and swung his arm back and forth. As Mimi stared, the arm swinging slowed, then stopped. But Lucy didn't let go. John Martin didn't make her, but he looked like a puppy that had just peed the rug.

"Guess you're over Lauralu," Mimi huffed.

Lucy dropped his hand like a hot rock. "Lauralu who?"

John Martin ducked his head toward her. "Ancient history," he whispered. She caught his hand again.

"Lauralu Meaks wanted to marry John Martin right after high school graduation," I said. "She dumped him when she heard how many years it took to become an engineer." When I said the word "marry" they both blushed. Mimi glared. At least no one was thinking about my homework anymore.

Lucy didn't even attempt to get in the cab when the truck was loaded. "You couldn't pay me to ride up front," she said, hopping in back with me. "This is way more fun." The truck bed had dried. The metal was hot through the butt of my overalls. Lucy took off her pale blue sweater and sat on it, like she didn't care she was going to get rust on it.

"How many sweaters do you have, anyway?" I shouted as we bumped out of the lot.

She looked up as if the sweaters were floating over her head. "Twelve? Fifteen? How about you?"

"I don't know." I had exactly two: the one Mimi had made, and a striped one I never wore because the stripes went the fat direction.

"Listen," she said. "If you want, I'll bring you one of mine. The color washes me out, but you could wear it. It'd go great with that chestnut hair of yours."

Chestnut? The only description I'd ever heard of my hair came from George Daniels, a popular creep in my class. Once he'd tugged the end of my braid, then dropped it. "Dog-crap brown," he'd said, wiping his hand on his pants. I grabbed the end of my braid, which was whipping in the wind, and took another look.

I was debating whether it was dog-crap brown or chestnut when Lucy started singing. "Somewhere over the rainbow…" I joined in. "…way up high." Between the wind and the rattling suspension they couldn't hear us up front. *I* could barely hear us. About the time we hit "Someday I'll wish upon a star…and wake up where the clouds are far behiiiiind meeeeeeee...," Lucy went off on some harmony, leaving me to hang onto the melody alone.

The truck slowed when we reached the dirt drive to the house, so we could hear ourselves. "If happy little bluebirds fly...beyond the rainbow, why, oh why, can't I?" We sang together in a miracle of harmony.

"We're good," said Lucy.

"*You* are, but I could probably never sound that good again."

"Sure you could."

I wasn't so sure. For Lucy miracles might be everyday things. For me they were pretty rare.

~

Lucy stood at the kitchen window watching John Martin. Head under the truck hood, he was tracking down a funny noise he'd heard on the way home—I wondered if maybe it was our singing. Mimi marched over and handed Lucy a knife and a potato. "Quit admiring the boy's fanny and peel some spuds." As Lucy gouged out big chunks, Mimi bit her lip. When she couldn't take it anymore she sputtered, "I said *peel* it, not *carve* it," and she took the knife and potato back.

Lucy watched Mimi a while. "May I try again, Mrs. Piermont? I think I get the idea." Mimi handed her the knife. Lucy picked up a potato and poked out a chunk the size of a gum ball. "Lord help us!" Mimi plucked at the front of her blouse to unglue it from her sweaty chest and watched the potato shrink.

"It's too hot to cook," I said. "Let's sit under the Rainbirds."

Mimi kicked her shoes off. "I'm ready. The garden don't need watering, but I sure do."

I ran upstairs and put on my suit, then covered it with a Tractor-Pull T-shirt of John Martin's. "Ready for the Rainbirds!"

Lucy raised her nonexistent eyebrows. "What are Rainbirds?"

"Come on," I said. "You'll see."

28

Leaves brushed my bare legs as we followed the dirt path. Lucy's jeans picked up seeds from the Spanish needle weeds. The garden gets all runaway at this time of year. I tugged at the too-small swimsuit that kept creeping up my butt, walking behind the others so Lucy wouldn't notice. Mimi plopped herself in a lawn chair by an overgrown hill of squash.

I turned on the faucet. The Rainbird sprinklers John Martin had mounted on poles chattered to life. *Chicka-chicka-chick.* Lucy jumped back as drops freckled her boots, then she kicked the boots off, peeled off her socks, and dove for a chair. Water sprayed over Mimi's splotchy pink arms and pattered loudly on the squash leaves. It trickled cool, down to my scalp.

We were lazing around, our hair going from bad to worse, when John Martin came thrashing down the path. "I got the potatoes peeled and boiling." He stopped to watch the falling water, then took off his ball cap. With a flick of the wrist, it sailed across the garden. He stepped into the nearest cone of falling water and stood, eyes closed, face turned up.

Lucy's wet blouse was sticking to her chest. She crossed her arms and watched John Martin. I usually think of my cousin as big and lunkish, but seeing the way Lucy looked at him, I looked again. What a shock. If this had been my first time of seeing him, I would have had to call him good looking. Hot even.

That is, if he wasn't my cousin.

Chapter 4
The Smile Mile

W hat gives?" John Martin said, setting down his fork. "You were sick last Thursday too." He leaned across the kitchen table and slapped a hand on my forehead. "No fever. Quit messing, Rox, let's go." He pushed his chair back and grabbed his ball cap.

He kissed Mimi on one cheek; I kissed the other. My body left the house as if it was being operated by remote control. Trapped in the truck, I willed the battery to be dead, but the engine started right up. I peered through the windshield. "Is it supposed to rain today?"

"Twenty percent chance," he said.

Twenty percent! I slumped in the seat. My only other hope was to get sent to the nurse's office. I tried a tentative cough. John Martin glared straight ahead and shifted into first. "And catch the bus this afternoon, okay?" John Martin's schedule was erratic. Some days he picked me up. Some days I took the bus.

Today it was the bus. The perfect end to a Smile-Mile day.

~

Annarose and I sat against the wall opposite the girls' locker room. Inside, the other girls were dressing out, switching their regular shorts for other shorts, changing socks and shirts. For them it was a chance to show off two outfits in one day. Luckily, dressing out was optional at our school. My best friend and I never did it. We would have rather died than strip down to bras and panties in front of a roomful of girls.

"Too bad going to the nurse didn't work out," said Annarose.

I had almost gotten away with spending third period in the nurse's office. I was within falling-over distance of the plastic couch when Mrs. Day, making a starchy, creaking sound, leaned toward me in her white uniform. "I notice there's a third period Thursday pattern to your illnesses, Roxanne. You need to make an appointment with the counselor." When I told her that any third period on any Thursday would be fine, she sent me straight to P.E.

Voices boomed in the boys' locker room, some high, some low. George Daniel's voice had gotten deep over the summer. I heard him razzing Mike Hayes for wearing boxers instead of briefs. "Man," Mike said, "I wouldn't be caught dead wearing tightie-whities." But I knew he'd have them by next gym class. What George says goes.

Charles sat on the floor opposite the boys' locker room. I could see that he was drawing kung fu fighters in the margins of his math book. He never dressed out either.

The three of us stiffened when Coach Keys strolled down the hall, but it was like we weren't there. He stuck his head in the guys' door. "Some time today," he barked. He rapped his knuckles on the girls' door. "Let's go, ladies."

Doors opened. Sneakers squeaked on linoleum. George twanged the elastic waist of Joelle's shorts. She punched his arm. Annarose, Charles, and I watched the parade go by, then fell in behind the others. Coach hit the bar on the door and the pack trotted out into the bright, dusty heat. We stayed at the back. None of us had a chance of winning. Our only goal was to be alive at the end of the mile.

~

"I'm getting a stitch in my side," I gasped. Annarose, who was puffing and blowing right along with me, turned her head to say something sympathetic.

"Save it, ladies!" Coach Keys yelled. "Pick it up, pick it up!" He clapped his hands. "Move! Move! Move!" he grunted.

"Which side is your appendix on?" I asked Annarose, thinking of John Martin's mother, who had died when hers ruptured. Coach scolded us with a quick blast on his whistle. Annarose picked up speed. I couldn't.

George Daniels and all the other popular creeps had already run their weekly Smile Mile and were lounging in the shade of a live oak. "Go, you lard bricks!" George encouraged. Sara Michaels and Joelle McBride lifted their silky hair and let it fall around their skinny shoulders. LaShondra Washington was practicing her double backflips. They all looked cool and comfortable, like movie stars.

The only ones sweating—and still thudding around the track—were Charles, because of his bad foot, and George's lard bricks: Grady Sheehan, Annarose Sneed, Freddy Haley, and me. Last year Charles came up with a name of his own for the five of us, the Outbacks—we were doing a unit on Australia. He said it made us sound wild and a little dangerous. What the heck, it was better than lard bricks. But holding my side as I ran I didn't feel wild and dangerous. I felt sweaty and sick. Don't let me be last, I begged silently, as the skinny girls followed us with their eyes.

"Shoelace!" Annarose called to Freddy. If he tripped and fell, the earth would shake like the age of dinosaurs was back. The kids under the tree would laugh, then feel superior because they were thin. As if being thin was some great accomplishment, like inventing the lightbulb.

Lace whipping, Freddy crossed the finish line in a cloud of dust.

"Way to go, big guy," wheezed Annarose.

He threw his arms up. A pitiful move. But Freddy wasn't signaling some pathetic triumph—like fastest mile by a kid the size of a refrigerator. One step over the line, his shoelace had tripped him.

Ca-rash! Return of the age of dinosaurs! The skinny girls under the tree tittered.

Annarose crossed next. She put her hands on her knees and swayed as if she might faint. Her glasses slid down her shiny nose and fell in the dirt. You'd think one of the thin people would pick them up for her, but it was the dead dinosaur, Freddy, who crawled over and retrieved them.

Grady thundered across the line. He stood next to Annarose, blowing like a horse.

I was almost last, but not quite. I could hear one more pair of sneakers pattering on the track. Charles was still behind me. If I beat him, all eyes would be on him coming in alone, not me. Then I saw George Daniels. He limped along, imitating Charles.

"Come on," I called to Charles. "We'll be last together." Our feet hit the line at the same instant. We stood there gasping like a couple of catfish tossed up on the bank, grinning at each other.

Coach Keys hit the button on his stopwatch, then shook his head. "A new record," he said, dropping the watch back into the pocket of his khakis. "The world's slowest mile." He was still shaking his head when Grady lifted his shirt to wipe his face.

"Ga-ross!" squealed Sara.

Oblivious, Grady kept wiping.

"Grady!" Coach smirked at the stretched white skin of Grady's belly. "That's some labonza ya got there, kid. Ya showing it off for the ladies?"

Grady peered over the edge of the shirt, then dropped it. "No sir."

Like a breeze stirring up dirt, Coach's word riffled through the group.

"Hey, Grady," George said. "Superior labonza."

"Lasagna labonza," Mike LaValley chimed in.

"Hey, la*bonz*inator!" wailed Dallas Murphy.

Charles snatched Dallas's shirt and pulled his face close. "Shut...up."

33

As Coach jerked Charles away Dallas hooted, "You're scarin' me, Chicken Boy!"

Coach Keys picked up the whistle that hung around his neck and blew it once. "You have time to mouth off, you have time to drop and give me twenty-five. Let's go, people."

The skinny kids dropped and began pumping up and down. The Outbacks groaned as we lowered ourselves slowly to the ground. Only Charles stood, his good fist clenched. Coach gave his shoulder a friendly shove with his fingertips. "You too, Ames." For a long moment, Charles stared through the hair that hung over his eyes.

Don't mouth off, I begged silently. If coach calls your house, your dad'll kill you.

Charles spat, then dropped to the ground. For him, push-ups meant doing most of the work with one arm. Slowly, painfully, he began. One...two...

"Miss Piermont," Coach said. "You think this is a show for your entertainment?"

I began my own private torture. Ooooone...twooooo...

"Are you going to be all right?" Annarose asked as my chin touched the dirt.

"No. If I drop dead, tell the paper Coach Keys murdered me."

"Oh, I don't think he's trying to kill us."

"Of course he's trying to kill us. He hates fat kids."

The school day didn't get any better as it went along. The final act, the bus ride home, took almost an hour because we had to go all over the county. Joelle and Sara shared a seat, with George right behind them, leaning on the seat back. Unless you count Mikey, an elementary school kid who always grabs the seat next to me when I ride, I sat by myself.

~

I had complained to Mimi about the Smile Mile the second week of school. "My handwriting's not so good," she said, "but if *you* write the excuse, *I'll* sign it." Forget that. Annarose's mom had already tried it.

The next week I decided to tell John Martin. He was smart. He'd think of something. "A little exercise won't hurt you any," he said. So I quit talking about it.

But early that evening when John Martin was running the rototiller in the last of the daylight and Mimi was watching TV, I told Lucy. I was showing her how to make bread, and the whole Smile Mile story came bubbling out.

"That gym teacher is compensating," she decided, pushing the bread dough around.

"Compensating for what?" I asked.

"You tell me." She punched the dough. "Maybe he wishes he was taller. Maybe he's losing his hair." She stuck out her lower lip and blew to get her bangs out of her eyes. "Maybe his wife bosses him around." *Wham!* She buried her other fist. The bangs slid back down. "It's simple psychology." She took a clothespin off the windowsill with a doughy hand and clipped her hair back with it. "He feels inadequate and he's taking it out on you."

I tried to look at Coach Keys Lucy's way: psychologically. Coach *was* short, and he always wore a ball cap, so he *might* be going bald.

But the possibility I liked best was the bossy wife. I imagined her as big. A lard brick. "Drop and give me twenty-five," she'd growl, and Coach would kiss the dirt.

Lucy took one last punch and pushed the dough ball toward me. "Your turn, Rox! Get out your frustrations."

I made a fist. *Whomp!*

"Harder!" cried Lucy, "Pretend it's Coach Keys."

I gave it another smack. "Right in the labonza!" I said, but Coach didn't have a labonza. In fact, he was pretty buff for an old guy— maybe it was all those push-ups he did for his lard-brick wife. All of a sudden, it was Grady Sheehan I was punching. As the cool, clammy dough sucked my fist in, I felt the air woof out of poor Grady.

"Way to go!" said Lucy.

"Yeah," I said. "But this isn't the way you knead bread." I gathered the dough back into a ball, squeezing out air pockets made by our knuckles. I pushed it with the heels of my hands, gave the ball a quarter turn and leaned into it again. I made the same motions over and over. As I worked the dough, I calmed down.

"Hey, can I do that?" Lucy asked.

"Okay. Just take it easy, Lucy. Get into a rhythm."

"Right. I tend to do things in bursts. Have you noticed?" She began to knead the way I had showed her, leaning on the heels of her hands, whistling a skinny tune between her teeth. "I can see why your mom liked doing this," she said after a while.

"What?" I turned my head so fast I slapped her shoulder with the end of my braid. "What did you say?"

"Johnny said she used to make bread all the time. Her name was Helen, right?"

"Right."

Hearing Lucy mention Helen was like the time John Martin told me he could see my imaginary friend Boo. When I quizzed him, my cousin described him all wrong, but for a second Boo was *really* real because someone else could see him.

"He said she made bread to get out her frustrations." She pushed the ball of dough back to me. "Sounds like your mom had quite a temper."

I had always imagined Helen as quiet, like me. I pictured her sneaking away when she left, slipping out the door before the rest of the house woke up, the sky just beginning to turn gray. But maybe she had stormed out, long brown hair streaming.

John Martin banged through the kitchen door and Lucy pranced over to him. He held up his hands. "Don't get too close. I been sweating like a horse; let me take a shower." But as he turned away, Lucy touched him with a doughy finger. She couldn't *not* touch him. While she trailed him with her eyes, I imagined my cousin chatting casually with her about my mother. I felt lousy. He should have told *me* if he told any one. I waited until he'd loped up the stairs. "What else did John Martin say about my mother?" I asked softly.

She screwed up her mouth, thinking. "Not much. He doesn't seem to want to talk about her."

That made me feel better. "If he ever does, could you tell me, please?" But I immediately wished I hadn't said it, because I wasn't one hundred percent sure I wanted to know. Too late. I'd unleashed Lucy.

She was scraping dough off her hands under the running tap but she stopped. "He hasn't told you about her? But Mimi has, right?"

"She always says she'll tell me sometime."

"Sometime?" She turned the tap off with a sharp twist and grabbed my upper arms with wet hands. "Helen is your *mother,* Rox. You have a right to know *everything* about her. There shouldn't be *any* secrets." Her pale, stubby lashes ringed her eyes like exclamation points. "What do you suppose it is they don't want you to know?" she whispered.

"Nothing." I wished she'd just drop it.

"Why did she leave? Did they tell you that much?"

Over the years I had caught glimpses in the things Mimi said and didn't say—dozens of possible reasons why Helen had left. I picked one off the top of the pile and threw it at Lucy. "She probably left because I was the ugliest baby ever born!"

Suddenly, I was being squeezed in a wet, wiry hug. "No way! That's the kind of idea you get when you're kept in the dark. Not knowing about your mom isn't good for you. If you don't know who *she* is, how can you know who *you* are?"

I thought I knew myself pretty well. Sure, I had questions about my mother, but Mimi would tell me sometime. I could wait.

"We'll have to pump Johnny for answers, that's all there is to it."

"You said he doesn't want to talk, and we can't make him."

"We can't *make* him talk, but we can make him *want* to talk."

"How?"

She leaned so close the clothespin on her bangs poked me in the forehead. "We'll reintroduce his head to his heart. It's been a long time since they've had a good conversation." She tapped the middle of my chest with one finger. "He's afraid to listen to what's in here, but I think he needs to."

Something told me it wasn't a great idea. My cousin probably had plenty of things he didn't want to think about, like his own absent parents. "Are you sure we should be messing around with his head and his heart? I mean, it might be bad for him. And anyway, I'm okay."

"Okay?" she said, crossing her arms. "I'd say you're in denial. And don't worry about your cousin. Johnny's like a big old house that's had the windows closed too long. It won't hurt him to let a little air and sunlight in."

Chapter 5
Waiting for a Star to Fall

I t's like she lives here," said Mimi. "It's like I have another kid on my hands."

John Martin kept his head down, shoveling in cornflakes.

I was still doing homework, but I wrote J. M. + L. E. on the edge of my assignment, drew a heart around it, and slid it toward my grandmother.

Mimi made a face and pushed it back. "Couldn't you just drive her out in the country and lose her somewheres?"

"No way!" I said. "John Martin's in *lo-ove.*"

"You mind if I kill this kid?" my cousin asked.

"Be my guest," Mimi said. She put a hand on his arm. "Seriously, couldn't you break up with her or something?"

John Martin shoved another spoonful of cereal in his mouth and kept chewing.

"No?" Mimi's hands shot up, palms raised, arm fat swinging. "Why not?"

John Martin set the spoon down. "Because I like her, okay? I like her."

"I knew it, I knew it," I sang.

"You have a death wish, Rox?" he asked, picking the spoon up again.

"You *like* her." Mimi fussed with a dishcloth, blotting up a slop of coffee on the table. "So, when's the wedding?"

His spoon clanged on the table. "All I said was I *like* her! That's all I said." He put his bowl on the floor for Milton and shoved his chair back. "Ya ready, Rox?"

"Isn't it kind of early?" I asked, but I pushed my chair back too.

Mimi heaved a gusty sigh. "Since you aren't going to break up with her, do you think her royal majesty would mind fish cakes for supper?"

John Martin kissed Mimi's cheek. "Lucy's not coming for supper."

"Not coming?" My grandmother covered her heart with her hand. "Why not? Did she break a foot?"

"No," he mumbled. "I'm taking her out for supper."

I leaned over to give Mimi's cheek a kiss. "What?" She turned her head so fast she almost gave my lips an Indian rub burn. "Taking her out for supper? Why?"

I left the room to get my pack so I was safely out of reach. "A hot date, Mimi," I called. "Bet he puts on that *man* perfume you gave him last Christmas."

When I came back into the room, John Martin's thumbs were hooked through a couple of the belt loops on his jeans. "What's the big deal?" he asked, drumming his fingers on his thighs. "People go out for supper all the time."

"*Rich* people," Mimi said. "If you have money to throw around, buy a pair of boots."

John Martin joked about his falling-apart work boots all the time. Once he called them his Jesus shoes—Mimi smacked him—then he held up a foot. "See what I mean, Ma. The sole is holy." But I'd noticed that in front of Lucy, he kept both boots on the floor.

"Tell you what you do," Mimi said, limping across the kitchen. She stuck her head in the freezer. "You buy the boots. And I'll feed you both for free." The fish cakes rattled as she showed him the box. "Your favorite. Mrs. Paul's, see?"

"I already asked her," he said.

"We could eat Spaghetti-Os and save the fish cakes for tomorrow," I said, putting my arms through the straps on my pack. I hate fish cakes, and fish cakes without John Martin and Lucy would be too depressing.

"We're having fish cakes," Mimi insisted as I went out the door. "Your cousin will just have to miss out."

John Martin gunned the truck engine. "Oooh. Going out for dinner," I said, starting right in on him. He took the turn out of the driveway so fast the hard candies on the dash scuttled from his side to mine. "You must really *love* her."

"Did I say love? Did you hear me say love? I said I *like* her. That's all I said." And he turned the wheel hard.

I snatched a butterscotch before it slid back his way. "But *how* do you like her? Is she a friend or a *girl*friend?"

His fingers tapped softly on the wheel.

I could tell Lucy hadn't asked him about Helen. John Martin and I were razzing each other, same as always. "If each of you pays for your own meal, then it's friend," I went on. "But you can't say you're taking someone out if they pay for themselves. And that's what you said. You said, 'I'm taking Lucy out for supper.'"

The fingers drummed louder. "I hear a fly buzzing," he said. "And I'm about to swat it."

I popped the butterscotch drop in my mouth.

"All this candy Mr. Tully sends you isn't good for you," he grumbled. Each time John Martin goes in Tully's hardware store Mr. Tully gives him a couple of candies for me. "Maybe I should to tell him to stop." But I knew my cousin was only getting back at me.

I sucked my candy until we stopped in front of the school. "John Martin?" The old bear lifted a paw off the steering wheel. "I have some money saved up. You can have it if you want. You could take Lucy someplace nice."

The paw gave me a gentle swat on the cheek. "I got it covered. Listen up in school today, okay? And Rox? Thanks for the offer."

A few dry leaves swirled, and the truck was gone. Oh, dread. I was even earlier than usual. It would be fifteen minutes before Annarose's bus came. I looked around. George and Nick were kicking a hacky

41

sack. Joelle and Sara were checking each other for split ends. I looked for Charles, who gets to school whenever his father feels like dropping him off. I guess he hadn't felt like it yet. No one seemed to see me as I walked toward the bench shoved up against the wall of the school. No one said hi. I sat, then noticed that the overalls that had looked okay when I put them on now had a stain on the stomach shaped like New Jersey; juice from breakfast, I guess.

I slid a paperback out of my pack, a romance novel off a ten-cent table at the Show. They're dumb, but I'm kind of hooked on them. I always tear the covers off. They're too embarrassing. The pictures on the front are always the same—some guy with his shirt off holding a woman who looks as if she just passed out.

Holding the book so it hid New Jersey, I opened to where I had left off, but I never focused my eyes on the page. John Martin likes Lucy Everhart, I thought. And suddenly, in my mind, a bare-chested John Martin was holding a swooning Lucy. Gag! I quickly replaced the R-rated picture with a family shot, one that included a grumpy Mimi, and me standing right beside Lucy, the two of us wearing the same color nail polish. I moved John Martin to a spot behind us, or maybe off to one side. Much better, I thought.

~

Miss Llewelyn gave the class her secret smile; she was about to reveal her latest Story Starter. Miss Llewelyn was new this year. She was still trying pretty hard. She had already had us describe our day if we woke up one morning and discovered we were dogs. I had imagined being Milton. Another time we had to write a paragraph answering this question: If you were a pair of shoes, what kind would you be? Half the guys wrote about foot odor. A more experienced teacher would have seen that coming. I was my cousin's boots, walking across the scaffolding at his construction job. Miss Llewelyn liked it.

I don't mind creative writing. It doesn't seem like work, and it's not like math, where answers are right or wrong.

"Imagine..." Miss Llewelyn paused, eyes twinkling. "Imagine your mother or father at your age. What did he or she look like? What did he or she like to do?"

I panicked. Except for her eye and hair color I didn't know what my mother looked like at my age or any other age. And my father was like the negative numbers the smart kids played around with in math: less than nothing.

"You have twenty minutes. Now, go!"

I wrote a sentence about my mother's long brown hair and erased it. I wrote about the pink barrette, erased it. I wrote and erased until the paper got all scuffed, like a couple of dogs had had a fight on it.

"Five minutes!" Miss Llewelyn sang out.

I still had nothing but the dogfight scuffs on my page.

Joelle McBride sat near the window, ankles crossed, blond hair shimmering in the light. She was writing and writing, dotting her *i*'s with little hearts.

"Roxanne?" said Miss Llewelyn. "Are you on task?"

I ripped out a fresh sheet of notebook paper, hating every single one of its pale blue lines. What a dumb assignment. Maybe when Lucy got John Martin's head and heart reconnected, I'd have something to write about. For now, I'd have to make something up.

"Time!" said Miss Llewelyn. "Who would like to share?" It seemed like a good time to scratch my ankle. I dove behind my desk, while Joelle almost broke her arm off waving it around. "Okay, Joelle. Why don't you go first?"

"My mother, Laura Brandt, was the prettiest girl in her class. She had long blond hair and blue eyes." And blah, blah, blah, blah.

Big news. Her mother was perfect too.

While Joelle bragged about her pretty mother I drew a dog. It was supposed to be Milton, but Milt has so much hair he looks kind of indistinct. Maybe if I tried something like a dachshund...

"Roxanne?"

I looked up. Every eye in the room was on me.

"Read your composition, please," said Miss Llewelyn.

43

I sit at the back so I won't get called on. Charles, Annarose, and I are all back there, blending with the bulletin boards. My other teachers understand the way it works. But Miss Llewelyn doesn't. She calls on me all the time. Week before last she asked me to read my essay on "The Person I Admire Most." Everyone who read before me had admired some star or dead president. Patrice Fogarty, who is very born-again, had written about Jesus. But I had admired Mimi. I described her sitting under the Rainbirds, dripping and smiling. I told about a Christmas before Grandpa Bill died when she made five kinds of pie. Miss Llewelyn raved. Everyone else stared at me like I was an alien. "I read last time," I said.

"About your grandmother. I remember. We'd like to hear from you this time too."

My voice felt stuck. I wasn't sure if anything would come out, but I stared at the crummy drawing of Milton on the otherwise blank sheet of paper and pretended to read. "My mother, Helen May Piermont, stepped on a rusty nail and got tetanus. She died at the age of ten. The end." The class was quiet.

Too quiet.

Then George called out, "If she died at ten, where'd you come from?"

Oh. I hadn't thought of that. "I thought we were making it up. This *is* creative writing, isn't it?"

Miss Llewelyn looked disappointed—the worst look in the teacher arsenal. "Roxanne, you're a talented writer. I know you can do better than that. Take the next twenty minutes and try again."

A talented writer. All at once I wanted to write something really good for her, but I had nothing to say. My best hope was that she would get into a rapture about similes or metaphors and forget to ask me for the assignment. In case she didn't I wrote:

Dear Miss Llewelyn,

I never knew my mother. She left me with my grandma when I was three months old. I don't even have a picture. I know you're new and all, and I'm sure you don't want to make anyone feel bad, but you should think before you give this kind of story starter.

Yours sincerely,
Roxanne Piermont

I folded the paper in half six times. That's as many times as you can fold a sheet of notebook paper. I put the lump in my pocket.

When the bell rang, Miss Llewelyn was singing the praises of alliteration. "Daniel drove Donna's dog to the doctor daily." I waited until the students at the front of the room stood, and then made for the door.

"Roxanne?" Her voice sailed over the sound of scraping chairs. "I need that assignment."

I turned slowly, fished the clump of folded paper out of my pocket, and swam against the tide of students to drop it on her desk. "Roxanne? What is this?"

I was out the door before she could unfold and read it.

~

Mimi shook her head at the pile of cold fish cakes on the platter. "So many leftovers." She'd eaten one. I'd eaten one. Neither of us likes fish cakes. Even Milton, who eats anything, including dirt, is just

45

so-so about fish cakes. John Martin is the only one who actually likes them.

"Can we at least have canned peaches for dessert?" I asked.

"Sure." Mimi scuffed over to the pantry and came back with a can and a can opener. "You do the honors."

I kept my eyes on the can I was opening. "I kind of like her," I said, not very loud.

Mimi threw up her hands. "First John Martin, now you. Is it contagious or something?"

I grinned. "If it is, you're next."

"Not me. I was perfectly happy not knowing her, thank you very much." She twisted the paper napkin in her hand. "But I guess this is what I have to look forward to. You two will grow up and get married and leave me here all by my lonesome." She looked as deflated as a birthday balloon two days after the party.

I rushed over and hugged her shoulders. "I'm not getting married, never, ever. And I won't go anywhere." I pressed my cheek against hers.

"Yes, you will, honey." Her fingers stroked my arm. "Sure you will."

"I'm only twelve."

"And next will come thirteen, then fourteen." She gave my arm a little slap as she said each number. "Before you know it you'll be eighteen, nineteen. Time flies."

"Come to my math class," I told her. "Mr. Brenner makes time stand still." As I rocked her gently back and forth she began to hum a song Grandpa Bill used to sing: "Casey Would Waltz with the Strawberry Blonde." He would dance Mimi around the kitchen, singing, while she laughed and called him an old fool. But I knew if I let her hum her way to my favorite part—"...his brain was so loaded it nearly exploded..."—she'd start talking about him and get even sadder.

"Want to work on our wreaths after we eat our peaches?" I asked.

The humming petered out. "May as well." She ran her fingers

over my arm so light it almost tickled. "At least until the boys start coming around and you get too busy for your old Mimi."

"No way. Guys are gross."

Her dry smoker's laugh rustled like paper. "Give 'em time. They'll start to look better."

She didn't know the guys in my class.

∼

We worked at the dining room table, which had vanished under a sea of craft supplies again. Since Lucy was a regular now, we'd gone back to eating in the kitchen. She wasn't company anymore, just one more dirty paper plate.

Mimi flattened the magazine with one hand and pushed it my way. "Read the directions, Rox. See how Martha makes her wreaths." Step one for Martha was ordering pinecones. John Martin and I had picked ours up off the ground out back. Step two called for wire. We had plenty. All we had to do was untangle it from the ribbons and string.

When I'd finished reading the directions, Mimi picked up the magazine and stared at the picture. "Martha's wreaths look puny. They need some glitter."

I edged pinecones with glue then sprinkled them with glitter-snow. Beautiful. Mimi wired them together. "What do you say, Rox?" She held up a finished wreath. "How much?"

"Twenty-five dollars, easy."

"Twenty-five, easy," she repeated, looking at me over her Dollar Store glasses. "Come on, Rox. We're talking about the Show."

"They're so beautiful. They must be worth twenty-five somewhere."

"Like where?"

"I don't know. Somewhere over the rainbow?"

"Sorry, Dorothy, but I'm afraid you're still in Kansas."

∼

Mimi was dozing in front of the TV, but woke herself up coughing. She blotted her eyes with a tissue and looked at the clock. "Ten-seventeen. How long can it take to eat supper?"

I rubbed my eyes and stretched. "Maybe they went to a movie."

"A movie?" Mimi threw up her hands. "Stop it! Isn't supper bad enough?"

"I'll wait up for him," I offered. "You go to bed."

"I wouldn't sleep a wink. I'd lie awake and worry."

"We'll both wait."

She glanced at the bushel baskets of grapes and gourds in the hall. John Martin and I had picked them before he went off to supper with Lucy. "At least one of us should be rested for the Show tomorrow," she said. "Go on, I'll watch a little more TV." She turned her cheek up for a kiss.

I crawled into bed, but left the door open a crack so I could see John Martin when he got home. Just looking at him I'd know the answer to the friend/girlfriend question.

John Martin cut the engine and coasted, but the sound of the truck pulling into the yard still woke me up. The clock by the bed said twelve.

Mimi must've fallen asleep in her chair. As the front door opened she made a sound like a surprised chicken.

I crept to my bedroom door. "You didn't need to wait up," I heard my cousin say.

"Of course I did. I had to be sure you got home safe."

"I'm twenty-three, Ma."

"You're still my boy."

"And I'm home now, so would you please go to bed? Come on. I'll give you a hand getting up the stairs."

"I can still make it by myself. Go to bed. I'll be up after a while."

"Holler if you need a shove." I heard him give her a kiss and walk away. The footsteps on the stairs were John Martin's.

"So, how was supper?" she called. "What did y'all have?"

Peering around the edge of the door, I saw his head. He was

almost at the top of the stairs. "It was fine. We had grouper."

"Fish?" Mimi sounded wounded. "You could've had fish here. I got a whole plate of fish cakes in the fridge."

"Good night, Ma. I love you." His chest appeared as he climbed another step.

"John Martin?" she called after him.

"What?" His head turned.

"There's straw all over your back."

"Yeah," he said, brushing at his shirt. "Lucy made me pull over at the edge of a field to look at the stars."

Mimi paused a beat. "Stars, huh?"

He pointed a finger at her. "You have a dirty mind, Ma."

"Me? I'm not the one with straw all over my back."

"It wasn't like that," he protested. "We were coming back here after supper when Lucy asked me if I wanted to see a falling star. So we pulled over next to Hodgkin's field."

"Lucky he didn't sic his dogs on you. Lucky he didn't come out with his rifle and shoot the both of you. How long were you out there?"

"I don't know. A couple of hours, I guess. It got pretty cold, but the sky was beautiful. We saw planes and a mess of satellites pass over."

"But did you see a shooting star?"

"She said she did, and I went along. I was freezing my tail off."

"I don't even know why I'm asking, but why was it so all-fired important to Miss Lucy that you see a shooting star tonight?"

"She says I think too much about the future, that sometimes I should live in the now." He rubbed his eyes. "Goodnight, Ma. This time I mean it." He stretched his long arms and pressed his palms against the ceiling above the stairs. "Boy, am I going to be whacked tomorrow, and we're tearing down walls." I was disappointed when the same-as-always John Martin climbed the last three steps. But then he stopped. He couldn't see me looking at him out of the dark, but I could see him—and smell his Christmas cologne.

49

Whatever he was thinking about lit him up like a jack-'o-lantern with a candle inside.

When he walked away I did a barefoot dance behind my door. Love! Definitely love! I bet he kissed her too. I felt happy, and then sad. Sad and happy both. I liked Lucy. Having Lucy around was like having a big sister or a great new friend, but John Martin in love was risky. If they got married, I guessed they might move into his room. But probably not. That was the risky part.

The only family I had that I could count on was Mimi and John Martin. I couldn't afford to lose either one of them.

Chapter 6
The Cool Test

They got that old look," Mimi complained when John Martin set a basket of grapes on the ground next to our sales table. "They look murky."

"Last of the season, Ma."

"Lucky the gourds are starting to come in," I said. "And the pumpkins." I scooted a few pumpkins toward the tailgate where he could reach them.

We'd planted pumpkins in the garden, but they didn't do half as well as the ones that had sprouted from a rotten pumpkin tossed on the compost heap. Vines crept down the sides of the pile and across the lawn, engulfing gnomes and saints in drifts of green leaves and yellow flowers. As the gnomes stared, the flowers had grown into pumpkins. I turned the pumpkins every few days so they'd get a nice even shape, and I kept count. Between the ones from the regular garden and the compost volunteers we had 48 large ones, 60 mediums, and a couple dozen smalls. And we only had two weekends before Halloween. Four days to sell 132 pumpkins.

Just like that, I switched from thinking about what was good about grapes to what was good about pumpkins. In sales you have to turn on a dime.

I got things set up, but it was pretty windy. "I can't find our tape," said Mimi, holding down one of my signs with an elbow. "Think you can borrow some?"

Mr. Finch dug a roll of masking tape out of the toolbox under his table. Today, along with incense, he was selling pipe cleaners. "For craft projects," he said, without much enthusiasm. "I got 'em cheap so I couldn't refuse. But what am I going to do with a whole gross?" He blew his nose. "One hundred and forty-four boxes of pipe cleaners. All black. You want some, free? Help yourself." I took four boxes.

Back at our booth, I made a pipe cleaner spider and twisted it around a pumpkin stem. "Does the spider come with it?" asked a woman who was trying to choose a pumpkin. When I said it did, she bought that one. I made more spiders. Marco tied one to a string and dangled it to scare his baby sister. Instead he scared his mom so bad she almost dropped the baby.

My spiders became a craze. Folks bought pumpkins just to get them.

I attached a spider to the elastic at the end of my braid and made a sign. "Spiders! The Halloween Accessory!" I began selling them separate.

At eleven, I went back to Mr. Finch for more pipe cleaners. For the past two hours, he had watched pipe cleaner spiders go by on the brims of men's cowboy hats, looped through buttonholes, and dangling from baby strollers. His red eyes peered at me through incense smoke. "No more free samples," he said, crossing his arms. I could tell he had put two and two together.

"Okay," I said, crossing my arms too. "How much for the whole gross? I don't need that many, but if the price is right I might take 'em off your hands."

Mr. Finch rocked back on his heels. "I don't know, girly. Make me an offer."

In two years at the Show I'd learned to start low, find out where the bottom is. "Five bucks for the rest of the gross."

"Pffffff..." he sputtered. "Don't insult me." But I could tell that five dollars wasn't too far from what he had paid for them. Mr. Finch was bluffing. I respected that.

"Seven," I said. "Plus I'll give you some spiders for your display."
His watery eyes narrowed. "How many spiders?"
"A dozen, plus a pumpkin."
"Two dozen," he countered. "And you keep the pumpkin."
We shook on it.

~

Carrying the bundle back to our display, I began planning. I would try to get rid of all the black pipe cleaners by Halloween. One hundred and thirty-eight pumpkins and a gross of black pipe cleaners. I needed more advertising. I attached spiders to my ears, my collar, and the straps of my overalls. A few more dangled from my hair. Marco stared open-mouthed. Mrs. Yu laughed and called me the spirit of Halloween.

And I sold spiders.

I had just made a spider necklace and hung it around my neck when I heard a sickeningly familiar voice. "Hey there, Spider Woman." I didn't turn right away. It was a voice from school, and I was supposed to have two days off from it.

"Rox?" The voice sounded less sure. "That *is* you, isn't it?"

I tried to act pleasantly surprised. "Oh. Hi, Joelle. What're you doing here?"

"My mom dragged me. What are *you* doing here?"

"I work here."

"You do? Wouldn't you rather baby-sit?" She was carrying some of Mr. Finch's incense, the deep magenta sticks he calls "Passion." When they burn they smell like underarm deodorant. Joelle lowered her voice. "There are some seriously weird people in some of the other booths," she said. "The old dude who sold me the incense kept snorting and hacking."

"Mr. Finch has allergies."

"And how about the honey lady?" Joelle held her breath and

puffed up her skinny cheeks. She took one look at me, and let the air out quick. "And the guy who sells the barnyard animals?" she rushed on. "He's missing half a hand."

"He got it caught in a hay bailer when—"

"I saw Charles Ames over there," she interrupted. "I guess he's working too. I don't know why, but he gave me these." She opened her hand.

I stared at a half dozen uranium green marbles. "Banshees. They're pretty expensive." I felt hollow. Charles had never given me banshees.

"But why did he give them to me?" she asked.

I shrugged. Because he has a dumb crush on you, I thought. Joelle was an idiot for not noticing the good in Charles Ames, and Charles was a jerk for not looking past the pretty outside to Joelle's rotten center.

She still held out the marbles. "What am I supposed to *do* with them?"

"Couldn't you just appreciate them?"

"Here, *you* appreciate them." And she dropped them into my hand. "How do you take it here, Rox? It's a freak show." Was this Joelle's way of being nice, implying that there were the freaks, and then there was her and me—not freaks? "Word of advice," she whispered. "Lose the spiders."

That did it. "For your information, Joelle, I have a job to do. Right now it's selling pumpkins." I was so mad, my voice shook. "If I don't sell them quick they rot." I couldn't believe I'd just said something about rotten pumpkins, but I rushed on. "Wearing spiders helps me sell." If we'd been at school I might have thought twice about Joelle's cosmic cool test. But this was *my* place. Me and my freaky friends were in charge here. "And these people are my friends, so watch your mouth."

She fell back a step, as if she had suddenly realized who she was talking to. Not the normal loser version of Roxanne Piermont, but a

Roxanne Piermont who wears pipe cleaner spiders all over her body—a girl who hangs out with freaks and likes it.

Mimi set down the chili dog she was eating, chili gobbing the corners of her mouth. "Aren't you going to introduce me to your school chum?"

"This is Joelle McBride."

Mimi stuck out a hand. Joelle pretended she didn't see it. "Nice to meet you. Gotta go. I think my mom is looking for me."

"What a pretty girl," said Mimi as Joelle made her escape.

Did being pretty make it okay to be mean, nasty, stuck-up, and snobby?

Mimi blotted her lips with a paper napkin. "Too bad she's such a little brat."

Good old Mimi.

~

"Wow," said Lucy, staring at my spiders. "Arachnophobia."

We were packing up for the night, but I stopped to hook a couple of them through her hoop earrings. "Look!" She spread her arms. "What do you say, Johnny? How about this fashion statement?"

John Martin whumped the pumpkins he was carrying down in the back of the truck. I thought he was too busy loading to look at her spider earrings, but he turned and let out a ghoulish cackle. "I vant to bite your neck," he said. Then, oh my gosh, he put his lips on her neck. I mean, he kissed her a wet one right in front of Mimi, in front of me, in front of the whole entire freak-show world!

Danny clapped. "Way to go, man! I was beginning to worry about you."

Marco giggled.

John Martin's ears went up in flames, but he was grinning. "What's the matter with you people? You never see a vampire attack before?" He hid his face in the crook of his elbow, as if he was pulling a cape around himself and let out another bloodthirsty cackle. He chased Lucy around and around the truck.

~

"He really likes you," I shouted at Lucy. We were up against the tail-gate, away from the back window of the cab so we could have some privacy, not that they would have heard us if we were closer. We had to scream our secrets in each other's ears. "I mean, really, really likes you."

"How can you tell?" she yelled.

"Because he's acting stupid."

She was so happy that John Martin was acting stupid she hugged me. Then she said, "I still haven't gotten a thing about your mom out of him." She frowned. "Sorry. But, hey, I brought you something." She crawled past the pumpkins and the last basket of grapes to grab a brown paper bag. "Here." She held it out. "Open it."

I unrolled the crinkled top and reached in. My hand brushed the softest thing I'd ever felt.

"It's that sweater I promised you," she shouted as I pulled it out. "Try it on."

The wind whipped the sleeves. The spiders in my hair got caught when I pulled it over my head. Lucy kept untangling things. She gave the front a quick tug, smoothed the shoulders, and then sat back. "Like the color? It's burgundy. *Your* color."

I stroked a sleeve. The sweater was too tight, but it felt furry and soft, like a pet. "I love the color!" I said, as I tried to figure out if I did. It wasn't a color Joelle would pick. She liked candy colors like pink and pale blue. I pulled the end of my braid over my shoulder. It was a miracle. The sweater changed the color of my hair from dog-crap brown to chestnut.

"You look drop-dead gorgeous," Lucy shouted.

I wasn't gorgeous; *it* was gorgeous. But maybe it would rub off.

Chapter 7
Sister Spider Knows All

Only a foot stuck out from under the blanket. "Brought your coffee," I said softly. The lump under the covers barely stirred. "Want me to cover your foot?"

"No," the lump answered. "That's my temperature regulator."

"Oh." I was still holding the coffee. "We have to leave for the Show soon."

Mimi groaned and flopped the covers back. "Check my tongue." I switched on the bedside lamp; she stuck her tongue out.

"Coated," I said.

"It feels like Mary's little lamb." The skin under her eyes was gray; her cheeks were damp and pale. She turned the light off. "You think you could do the Show alone, Rox? If you have to pee, just take the cash with you. Get Danny or Mrs. Yu to keep an eye on things." She reached out and squeezed my hand. "You're the one who does most of the selling anyway."

I heard John Martin's boots on the stairs. "Getting late, Ma. Rise and shine." He stood in the doorway, the hall light on behind him. Steam rose from his coffee cup. Hat on backwards, he was ready to go.

"Mimi's sick," I said.

"Sick?" He lumbered into the room and put a hand on her forehead, his only test for illness. "No fever."

"I'm not *that* kind of sick," she said. "Now, would you take this child to the Show? It's getting late."

A floorboard creaked as John Martin shifted his weight. "She's twelve, Ma. I can't drop her off and leave her. I'm sure there's a law, child labor or something. And you know I can't stay with her. I have to get to work."

"Give me ten minutes." Mimi struggled up on her elbows then swooned back. "My word! So that's what they mean about seeing stars."

"Skip the Show for one day," he said. "Rox should be home studying anyhow."

"No!" I said. "The pumpkins will go bad." Not to mention the gross of black pipe cleaners I had to sell by Halloween.

My grandmother closed her eyes. "What about Lucy?"

"What *about* Lucy?" he asked.

She opened one tired eye. "For a smart boy you're thick as a post. She eats here. She goes through groceries like she was a member of the family. Would it kill her to do the Show with Rox?"

~

I was finishing the setup when John Martin brought Lucy back. "You saved me from a terrible fate," she said, bounding out of the truck.

"What terrible fate?" I asked.

"Studying," said John Martin, who was carrying her books. He put them under the table next to mine, looked back and forth between the two of us, and left.

As he drove off Lucy grimaced. "We'd better study. If we expect John Martin to get in touch with his heart, I guess the two of us can get in touch with our heads." She checked the gold watch on her wrist. "We'll start at eleven, no matter what."

"No matter what." It was easy to agree. Eleven was three hours away.

I taught her to make spiders. Soon we were both decked out. But Lucy had her own promotional idea. "Buy a pumpkin, get a fortune free," she bawled. "Sister Spider sees all! Knows all! Tells all!"

Danny had given us donuts, so she read his palm without a pumpkin sale. "I see romance in your future."

"Sure." Danny hooked his thumb in the waist of his jeans. "Always."

"Wait!" she shrieked, snatching his hand back. "This is serious! I see a blonde..." She looked up at him. "No, a redhead."

"Yeah, Tina."

"I also see jewelry. Could it be a ring?"

"W-what?" he stammered. "Show me where it says that!"

Mrs. Yu's palm had to be read too, since she was a special friend of Mimi's. "I see something brand new on the way. It is very small, but it is worth its weight in gold."

Mrs. Yu clapped her hands. "A grandbaby!" She went back to her racks of party dresses and started looking at the baby sizes.

"Buy a pumpkin, get a fortune free," Lucy called. "Sister Spider knows all!"

I noticed that the people whose palms Lucy read often looked startled, as if she had named the very thing they wanted most, something hidden deep in their hearts they thought only they knew.

"You're a good palm reader," I said, wondering what was hidden in my own palm.

"It's not hard." She glanced at her watch. "Eleven on the dot, Rox. Let's go."

Lucy was about to learn why my teachers always put little notes saying *Watch penmanship!* on my papers. Knees make lousy desks. She had barely opened her book when a man in greasy jeans said, "Hey, I'm here for the free palm reading."

"Free if you buy a pumpkin," Lucy said.

He bought a bitty one-dollar pumpkin and held out his hand. "There are two women who love you," she said. Hard to believe, since his front teeth were missing, but I guess it was true if Lucy said so. "Pay special attention to the taller one," she advised. Then she said the window to the beyond had gone dark. It was a jiffy-presto

59

fortune—what did he expect, he only bought a dollar pumpkin—
but he wasn't satisfied with it.

She was trying to find her place in the book. "Why should I pay
attention to the taller one?" he asked.

"Your palm doesn't give details."

"Well, that's not much help, is it?"

"Enjoy your pumpkin...*and* your free spider. Have a nice day,"
she called after him. Lucy had the right attitude for sales. Maybe we'd
go into partnership. I was getting the idea she hated to study as much
as I did.

I was in the middle of World War I when I happened to look up.
Charles was just standing there. He had probably been there a while,
waiting to be noticed. "Mind if I hang with you a while?" he asked.
"My dad is ticked."

I fingered the banshees that were still in my pocket from the day
before and thought about Joelle. "Okay, I guess." I wanted to throw
the marbles at him, but I didn't. Getting them back would fix his stupid crush; it might break something else, though.

He slouched over to our side of the table, pressed his back against
a roof pole, and slid down.

"This is Lucy," I said.

"John Martin's girlfriend," she added, and she leaned down and
stuck out her right hand. Charles hesitated. He lifted his twisted
right hand, then changed his mind and gave her the left.

Lucy dropped to her heels, picked up both hands, and examined
them.

"Cerebral palsy," he said.

"Tough break. Do you suppose you would've been right-handed?"

"Oh, yeah, definitely. I have the world's worst handwriting, don't
I, Rox?"

"Pretty bad," I agreed. *Unbelievable.* Charles was talking about his
hand. He usually kept it hidden. The first time I saw a picture of
Napoleon with his hand inside his shirt, I thought of Charles.

"Get her to read your palm," I suggested. Then I remembered

that she had asked all her customers whether they were right- or left-handed; that was the hand she always read.

"Which hand should you look at?" I asked. "He's left-handed, but he should've been right-handed."

"The left," she said. "That's the life he's living. Let's see what your future holds, Charles." She sat cross-legged in front of him and opened his hand in her lap. "Wow!" She pulled back and turned away as if what she had seen was blinding.

"Shit!" Charles pulled back too. "I die young, right?"

"No. Your lifeline looks good and long. But get a load of this." She traced a line with her finger. "This is your head line. I've never seen one this deep. Charles, you must be a genius."

"Yeah, right. I stayed back last year."

She peered into his hand again. "I can see you don't like school. You feel uncomfortable, misunderstood, but you're plenty smart."

He took a closer look at his own palm. "All that's in there?"

"All in there."

He tucked his hands under his arms. "Well, it's wrong. I'm not smart. And why would lines in your hand be able to tell you anything anyway? They're just wrinkles."

"There you go," said Lucy, taking his hand back. "You're skeptical, a sign of true intelligence." He tried to make her let go, but Lucy hung on. "Let me check something." She angled his hand to catch the light. "Congratulations, Charles! I see college in your future."

Charles panicked. "No way! I'm dropping out the first chance I get. Those stupid wrinkles can't make me stay in school."

"Let's go back to the lifeline," she said soothingly. "Here's where you are now." She pointed at a spot where bunches of little wrinkles crossed. "You're confused."

"Not confused enough to stay in school," he mumbled.

"Things are going to change. See, things straighten out up here. Smooth sailing."

"Really?" He flicked the long hair out of his eyes so he could take a good look at the clear line of his future.

"Wait! Wait!" yelled Lucy.

Charles about jumped out of his skin. "What? I get hit by a truck?"

"No. I just took a look at your heart line…"

"Nothing, right?"

"Au contraire, monsieur!" She wiggled her eyebrows. "Va-voom!"

He put his hands back into his armpits and glared. "You making fun of me?"

"No. You're going to be a serious ladies' man, Charles."

He lurched to his feet. "Now I *know* it's all a crock. And I'm not going to college either." Charles seemed to be falling forward as much as walking, barely catching himself with each step. He ran into our table, then into a boy eating peanuts. I wanted to chase after him, but what could I say? We watched until he disappeared in the crowd. Still kneeling on the ground, Lucy hung her head. "Lucy girl, you really blew it that time. But Rox, why wouldn't girls like him? He's cute. He's nice."

"He walks funny." I squeezed the marbles in my pocket. "Most girls notice things like that."

"Most girls are stupid," she said. "By the way, I think he has a little crush on you, Rox."

I let the marbles fall to the bottom of my pocket. "Trust me, he doesn't."

"I could take a look at your palm—"

"Did you really see college in his hand?"

"Sure." She stood and slapped the knees of her jeans, but the smudges from the dirty floor stayed. "Charles needs to go to college, so of course I did."

"But you saw it in the wrinkles, right?"

"They're just wrinkles, Rox."

"But…but you knew so much about everyone. You must see *something.*"

"It's not hard to guess what people want. It's simple psychology— even if I've never had a course."

I had been about to ask her to read my palm, not to look for a dumb crush Charles didn't have on me, but to see if somewhere in the future I'd be skinny and do okay in school, if some time I'd meet my mother. There was no point in asking now. It was all made up. Like Charles said, a crock.

Chapter 8
Something Waiting in the Dark

Hey, Dandruff Man!" Lucy yelled as John Martin climbed out of the truck. He was dusty all over. "What have you been up to?" she asked. Only the skin around his nose and mouth, which had been covered with a mask, was normal.

"Tearing out plaster." Dandruff Man walked over and kissed her with his undusty lips.

I felt kind of squeezy seeing John Martin kiss Lucy. After spending the day with her, she seemed more like my friend than his girlfriend. "We got our homework done," I said.

"Both of you?" he asked.

She rolled her eyes. "Of course, both of us."

She got another kiss. I got a slap on the butt. "Could we pack up and go?" I asked, returning the slap, with interest. "I want to check on Mimi."

~

Mimi snatched her teeth out of the pocket of Grandpa Bill's old terry robe and put them in quick. "I didn't hear y'all drive up."

John Martin kissed her cheek. "Feeling better, Ma?"

"Better?" She stared into the cup of tea in front of her on the kitchen table. The paper tag and string had fallen in; she let them float. "Better than what?"

"Better than this morning."

She waved a hand like the question was a mosquito. "I have a funny pain in my stomach. My feet feel numb. I'm fine."

John Martin flexed his tired shoulders. "That's good."

Lucy turned on him. "What do you mean, good? You need to see a doctor, Mrs. Piermont. Right away."

"Why? To hear Doc Winslow say I'm old and I smoke too much and I need to lose a few? Why pay forty bucks to hear what I already know?"

Lucy spun a chair on one leg and straddled it. "Numb feet could be serious." She gripped the top of the chair with both hands. "It sure isn't normal."

"Not for you, maybe, but welcome to my world." Mimi pushed a sleeve up to keep the cuff dry and fished the tea bag out of her cup. "Get to be my age, Lucy, you'll see. Every day it's something."

"Have you had a recent physical, Mrs. Piermont?"

"Physical schmizical. C'mere." She lifted Lucy's hand off the back of the chair, and held it. "Let me tell you about the golden years, Lucy. You get lumpy and ugly and your parts begin to quit on you. You put your teeth in a glass at night. You can't remember where you set stuff down. And one day you forget to wake up. Good-bye, earthly plain. Heaven, here I come. It could happen any time." She tried to drop Lucy's hand, but Lucy held on.

"Anytime? Let's just see if that's true, Mrs. Piermont." And Lucy pinned Mimi's hand, palm up, on the table. She nodded, then clucked her tongue. "I'm afraid you're stuck on the earthly plain for a while more." She ran a purple nail along the furrow in the middle of my grandmother's hand. "You have a long lifeline."

Mimi squirmed. "Stop it. That tickles." Then she peered into her own hand. "How long is long?"

"Very. This is your husband's death, right here."

Mimi stared at the spot where the line split. "So that's Bill going off. Bye-bye, honey. How much time do I have after that?"

"Twenty-five years. Thirty years. See, it wraps all the way around

65

your thumb to the back of your hand. You'll get to see John Martin become an engineer and Rox go to college." She got a mischievous smile. "My, my. Eight babies."

John Martin was pouring the last little bit of coffee out of his thermos into a cup. "Eight?" he squeaked, dribbling coffee onto the table.

"Sorry, Johnny, I'm wrong about that. Nine. Nine babies."

The corners of Mimi's mouth twinked up. "You better be a good engineer. That's a lot of kids to keep in shoes."

He paused with the coffee cup halfway to his lips. "Some are Rox's, right?"

Lucy smiled at him. "Of course. Only seven of them are yours."

But Mimi was thinking about her long, long lifeline. She turned her hand over. "Wraps right around the thumb, don't it?" She heaved a sigh. "Makes me tired just thinking about it. I'm going back to bed." She dragged herself up the steps, followed closely by Dandruff Man, who needed a shower.

~

"Show me your room," Lucy whispered. "It used to be your mother's, didn't it?" We followed my cousin's dust trail up the steps. "I keep asking, but Johnny hasn't cracked yet. Maybe we can find something."

"I'll show you what I've found so far." I opened my closet door and took the shoe box off the shelf.

Lucy stared into the old Keds box. "This is everything you have from your mother?"

There was the plastic barrette, a tube of Bonnie Belle lipstick, the spelling list, the brush that might have been Helen's—although the hair that was in it looked suspiciously like dog. "This is pitiful." Lucy shook her head as she put the lid back on. "You have to ask your grandmother. You have a right to know."

"Mimi says kids don't have rights." I flopped back on my bed and stared at the water stains on the ceiling, wishing Lucy would drop the whole thing.

I heard hangers slide. "Why do you have all these men's clothes in your closet?"

"They're Grandpa's," I said. "Mimi couldn't bear to part with them."

"Maybe she still has your mom's stuff somewhere too. We should look around."

We could look, but I knew there was nothing to find. Mimi gets rid of anything she doesn't want to think about.

"Hey, Rox!" Lucy sounded excited. "What's that?"

I pushed up on my elbows. She had just tipped the box back onto the shelf, but she was still on her toes, looking up. I knew she hadn't found anything on the shelf. I'd looked a hundred million times. All I'd ever found were spiders, some dead, some live.

"There's something in the ceiling. It looks like a trap door!"

"Oh, that. That goes into the attic, but Mimi never puts anything up there."

"Have you ever looked?"

"I can't reach it. And anyway, I told you, there's nothing up there."

Lucy took a little jump, making the trap door clatter as it lifted and dropped back into place. "Do you have a flashlight?"

"Sure." I kept a flashlight in my sock drawer for reading under the covers. As I handed it to Lucy, she gripped my wrist with her free hand and pulled me into the closet too.

"Here, you hold the light, and I'll try to open it."

"Okay," I said. We were both whispering, even though Milton was the only one who could hear us.

Lucy went up on tiptoes again and pressed her fingers against the board. Musty air hit my face. It smelled like dust and things left in the dark. *Scrape.* She pushed the hatch to one side and reached in, but she could only feel around the very edge. "Have anything I can stand on?" she asked, wiping her fingers on her jeans.

The 1952 *World Book Encyclopedia* sat in a dark wooden case by my bed. It took Aardvark through Gypsum to raise Lucy high enough to poke her head through the hole.

"Hand me the flashlight," she said.

"Anything?" I asked when she'd shined the light around a few seconds.

"Squirrel turds," she reported. "And some kind of small skeleton—probably squirrel."

"Anything else?"

She jumped up and hung by her elbows, her chest and head through the hole. "There are the sides of a yellow crib. A box of moldy stuffed animals... Wait! There's something on the other side of this beam. I can't...quite...reach..." With each kick more of her disappeared. "Got it!"

"What is it?" I felt suddenly breathless.

"I'm not sure." She pointed her toes, feeling around for the encyclopedias. I hugged her shins and tried to guide her feet. As her toes touched, the pile teetered. Lucy went down in a whoosh of cascading books. I fell back into the room, landing on my butt. When the crash was over, only her boots stuck out the closet door.

"Lucy! Lucy, are you okay?" The hand that emerged from between the hanging clothes held a small book. "What's that?" My heart was beating funny. The small, dust-covered book was closed with a strap and a lock. I took it in both hands and blew across it; I wiped it with a sleeve. The cover was blue. I wiped it again and gold letters shimmered faintly. "Lucy!" I breathed. "It's a diary."

Lucy parted the clothes and gave me a thumbs-up. "Jackpot."

"But it's locked."

"No biggie. I'll get a knife," Lucy said, crawling out. "We'll cut the strap."

To me it was as if my mother—my real mother, not the one I'd made up out of a single barrette and a spelling list—was waiting behind the cover. Now that I actually had the chance, I was afraid to meet her. "No, wait. We've got a jar of old keys downstairs. I'll bet one of them would fit it."

"Why waste time? Let's bust it open."

Once when Annarose was spending the night, we snuck Mimi's *National Enquirer* up to my room and read about Michael Jackson's alien love child and the barking dog boy. We laughed so hard the soda Annarose was drinking came out her nose. Then Annarose said maybe laughing at sad stuff like the dog boy was a sin. Would sharing the diary be like that, Lucy and me laughing when we shouldn't? I hugged the dingy book. "I don't know, Lucy. Maybe I should read it by myself first."

Her bangs flared as she blew out in frustration. "But Rox..." Then she must have thought about it psychologically. "No. You're right. This is your private journey." She squeezed my shoulders and gave me a shake. "But when you *do* feel like sharing, remember who helped you find it."

∽

John Martin flipped the sandwiches in the pan and pressed them with the spatula. He stirred the macaroni. He made grilled cheese and macaroni every time Mimi felt too bad to cook. I realized that we'd been having my cousin's grilled cheese pretty often lately. I could hear the laugh track from the TV in Mimi's room, and Mimi's dry cough. It sounded about the same as always. If Mimi could stay the same amount of sick, that would be all right.

Just as long as she never got worse.

"You girls are awful quiet," my cousin said, flopping a sandwich onto my plate. I had been thinking about my mother's diary, hidden in my underwear drawer. I wasn't sure I wanted to open it. He tipped the pot and rubbery white macaroni spilled out next to the sandwich. "What were you two up to in Rox's room just now?"

"Nothing," I said, spooning a glob of margarine onto the noodles.

He raised his eyebrows at Lucy. "Nothing?"

"Absolutely nothing," she said.

"Oh, I get it. Girl stuff." Then he ran up the steps with Mimi's sandwich on a plate.

"Did you take a look at those keys?" she whispered.

"All too big," I said.

"Try a bobby pin. I saw some on the back of the toilet tank. Poke one in the lock. It works sometimes."

~

I waited until the house was asleep before turning on the flashlight under my blanket. At the foot of the bed Milton burbled in his sleep, stretched, and rolled on his back. I pulled the bobby pin off the hem of my nightshirt. If the diary opened easy, I'd read it. If it didn't, I'd put it back in my drawer.

I straightened the pin and stuck one end in the keyhole and poked it around. Nothing happened. Maybe there was dust in there. I blew in the lock and tried again. When that didn't work, I pulled the strap from side to side to make the catch let go. It was a cheap diary; the leather cover was actually plastic, but it wouldn't open.

Forget putting it away! One way or another, I was going to open it. I hid the diary under the covers, then crept down the steps. Moonlight sparkled on the glittery pinecone wreaths. The bowl of silver sequins was a brilliant pool of light.

I had to find an Exacto knife to cut the strap. Feeling around for it, I knocked the glue gun on the floor. My heart pounded. I waited for a light to come on and the slap of John Martin's big, bare feet in the hall.

I was so busy expecting him to come down the stairs that I about had a heart attack when headlights shot through the window. Then I recognized the whine of the truck; John Martin was coming back from taking Lucy home. I was about to bolt for the stairs when the beam of light glinted on the knife. As I grabbed it, the headlights died. I was in the living room when I heard John Martin's key in the door. I ducked into the kitchen, hiked up my nightshirt, and stuck the Exacto knife in the elastic of my underpants.

I was filling a glass of water at the kitchen sink when John Martin came in. "Mimi needed a drink," I said.

He frowned. "Is she coughing again?"

"She says her throat is dry." I leaned to turn off the faucet and jumped a mile.

"You okay, Rox?"

"Muscle twinge," I gasped.

"Don't forget the ice," he said.

"Two cubes," we said together.

My cousin stared as I moved stiffly to the refrigerator.

"That must be some twinge," he said.

I banged the ice cube tray, dropped two cubes in the glass, and returned the tray to the freezer. I stood, holding the glass of water. There was nothing else to do but go up the stairs, and I wasn't sure I could do it without taking out my own appendix. I leaned against the refrigerator, feeling it hum. "I'll just rest a second."

"Come on." He turned and offered me his back. "Jump on. I'll carry you."

"I'll be okay in a minute. It's just a cramp."

"A cramp." He blushed. "Oh."

"Not *that* kind of cramp!" I blushed too.

He ducked his head. "Night, Rox." I listened to him sprint up the stairs two at a time.

I got over the cramp as soon as I heard his door close. I pulled up my nightshirt and retrieved the knife. When I got to my room I shined the flashlight on my stomach, but the prick from the blade hadn't broken the skin. Lucky thing I'd worn down the tip cutting cardboard.

I was about to dump the water in the bathroom sink when Mimi started coughing.

"Brought you some water," I said, slipping into her room.

The Jesus night-light by her bed lit the edges of her frowzled hair and her nose, but her open, toothless mouth was a black hole. She twitched, and coughed again.

"Mimi?" I whispered. Her eyelids fluttered. "I brought you water."

When she didn't raise a hand to take it, I held the glass to her lips. Water ran down the wrinkles next to her mouth. I blotted her with a tissue from the box on the nightstand, and she smiled a toothless-baby smile. "You're a good girl, Rox."

I pulled the blanket up to her chin. "You're a good girl too," I said.

I slid back into my room, heart pounding, and picked up the knife. It was time to open the diary.

Chapter 9
Ellie

HELEN MAY PIERMONT: AGE 13
THIS IS HER BOOK
1986

Warning: if you read this Spud you'll definately find snakes
in your bed. POIZON ONES!!!

She had filled in her name on the line in very careful handwriting. Like Joelle, she dotted the *i* with a heart.

"Thirteen," I whispered. "One year older than me." This diary would tell me what she was like in middle school, not the stuff Mimi was saving for later. Helen probably hadn't even kept it for the whole year. John Martin gave me a diary one Christmas. I wrote every day for maybe a week and a half. By April the diary was under the bed, the key lost, and most of the pages still blank.

I opened the back cover of my mother's diary so I could flip the pages and see how far she'd gotten. "Whoa!" The inside was filled with guys' names and initials. Robert Talmadge. "Robbie." Mrs. Robert Talmadge. Mrs. Helen May Talmadge. Everything about Robert Talmadge had been crossed out. Over the Mrs. Helen May Talmadge she had written *Don't make me puke!!!!* But there were plenty of other names. *C. J. 4ever. Roberto. Eddie Van Halen rocks!!!!* *Eric Hoffman. Andrew Harvest.* A tiny *JB* was encircled by a heart—

he must've been a quick one. Every other name had been written at least five different ways.

Then I noticed that Helen had crossed out the dates at the tops of the pages and written in new ones. I found the last entry. It was dated August 22, 1990. Wait a minute. I was born in 1990! When she wrote that I was three months old.

I closed the diary with a snap.

Everything inside me began fist-fighting: the blood and guts, the things that pumped and throbbed, the red arteries and blue veins. All I had to do was read and I'd know the story Mimi was always putting off until later.

What if Mimi had a good reason for waiting? I held the diary tightly shut. Maybe if I read it slowly…a couple pages a night…I could stop at any time.

I opened the cover and held the first page to my nose. It smelled like sunshine on a tar road, windowsill dust, the Cherokee roses that smother the fence around the garden. Normal stuff. Not scary at all. I lowered the diary and began again. *Helen May Piermont: age 13, This is her book, 1986.* I reread the warning to someone named Spud about snakes.

I picked up a pencil and lightly traced her letters. Her handwriting was nothing like mine, but it was comfortable to trace. She must've been a lefty, like me. I turned the page to the first entry.

January 1, 1986
Dear Diary,

Let me say right off I wish I got a radio or press on nails instead of this dum diary. I hate to rite and whats there to rite about? Nothing ever happens round here!

School starts tomorrow and I have to ware the stupid sweater Ma made. I hate it!!!!! Who wants to ware a blanket there mother made? Laura will laugh her butt off. Couldn't Ma at least of picked pink?

74

My New Years Revolutions:
1. grow my hair to the middle of my back
2. quit chewing nails
3. fix caterpilar eyebrows
4. get darling Robbie to like me
5. kill Spud

Who was darling Robbie? I checked the inside cover. Oh, yeah. Robbie Talmadge, the one who was going to make her puke. And Spud? He was the guy who was going to have poison snakes in his bed. "Well, that should kill him," I told Milton, who was snoring by my feet.

I got my notebook out of my pack and started a list of what I had learned about my mother. **Left-handed like me.** On the next line I wrote **Same sweater.** She hadn't described hers, but Mimi only makes one kind. I felt bad she didn't like the sweater and hoped she didn't tell Mimi, but she sounded like the kind of person who would. **Loves pink.** I know girls are supposed to love pink—Joelle loves pink—but I think it's wimpy. I wished Helen had picked my color, burgundy.

At least we were both left-handed. That was something.

On the next line I wrote **Terrible speller.** After reading a page from her diary, I was surprised she had only misspelled two words on her spelling list.

Next I wrote **Caterpillar eyebrows.** Then I went to the mirror over my bureau and shined the flashlight on my face. I would probably have noticed before if I had caterpillar eyebrows, but it didn't hurt to check. "No, no caterpillars." I scrambled back into bed and put the blanket over my head again. Neither Mimi nor Grandpa Bill had bushy eyebrows, so I added **Must skip a generation.** I held my breath and turned the page.

January 2
Dear Diary,

Ma had a cow. I hid the sweater behind a bush by the bus stop. I ment to go back for it, but when I got off the bus it was gone. I said I left it at school. She said no you didn't cause Johnny found it. Then she told me I was going to rot my teeth with lying and go strate to hell. Hell can't be no worse than here I yelled. Spud made himself scarce all afternoon. When I get ahold of him I'm gonna take care of revolution #5.

—Helen

p. s. Robbie stayed home sick today. Boo hoo!

I added **Liar** and **Sassy** to my list. "Mimi listens if you just talk to her," I said. "And couldn't you at least have pretended you liked the sweater?" I read the entry again and this time I laughed. I'd figured something out. Johnny had to be John Martin. And if Johnny was John Martin, then so was Spud. Boy would I like to ride him about that! Too bad anything from the diary had to stay secret.

I had read two pages, but I gave myself permission to read the next one too because it was right opposite. After that I would stop. Helen had already started to slide by the third entry. She had crossed out the date at the top of the page and changed the third to the fifth.

January 5
Dear Diary,

Its friday not that it matters. I have to turn in the first draft of Edison on Monday. I have to go to the library cause I need five sources. Ma says the World Book should be good enuff cause it has a page and a half about him and the print is small. She don't understand about bibliografies. Maybe Pop will take me. Robbie's working on his report there tomorrow. He said maybe I'll see ya.

Used Ma's tweezers to work on the caterpilars. Yow!!!

—suffering for beauty Helen

In my notebook I wrote **Edison report never dies (she did it before I was born, I'm doing it now)**. The only difference was in the old days it must've been an eighth grade project.

I closed the diary. So far my mother seemed like someone I could sit next to in class. I wondered what grade she got on Edison, and whether she ever made it to the library. I know I hadn't. Mimi still doesn't understand about bibliographies.

~

A knock on the door and John Martin bellowing his usual "Rise and shine" woke me. Everything was the same as always: John Martin's wake-up call, the light through the curtains, Milton sleeping in his favorite paws-up position. Then I slid my hand under the pillow and found the diary. Suddenly things seemed different. I told myself that was stupid. The first three entries had been nothing, but what about later in the diary when Helen was older? I could practically hear Lucy: What if there's something in there you *need* to know? Okay, Lucy, I thought. I'll read the next page. But then I have to get dressed for school.

January 7
Dear Diary,

At church Reverent Brown blabbed on and on and rolled his eyes up like he was looking through the floor boards of heaven. Its the same every week—like reruns. Why even go? But Ma says God keeps some kind of list of who comes. Being God must be a drag. All I could see of Robbie was the back of his head.

During fellowship Lynda said she had her five sources. She'll lend them to me if I walk over. Of course she's all done with Edison draft one. I haven't started yet. I saved Robbie a seat but he skipped fellowship to go squirrel hunting with his uncle.

—Edison Hater Helen

I closed the diary and picked up my notebook quick. **Felt the same as me about church,** I scribbled, and stuffed the notebook in my pack. I thought it over as I hunted for clean socks and underwear. Actually, I didn't mind church *that* much. We used to go all the time. Living far away from everything like we do, it was a chance to see friends on the weekend. You could tell we were members in good standing of Higher Praise Church when Grandpa Bill died; we ate church-lady casseroles for weeks on end. But without Grandpa, Mimi seemed to lose interest in God and everything else. Then, when money got tight we started doing the Show. Saturdays at first, then Sundays too.

"Rox?" my cousin yelled up the stairs. "I don't hear you moving around up there."

"I'm up," I said, pulling on a sock.

I still remembered one afternoon after we started doing Sundays at the Show. Some women from Higher Praise came to see Mimi about why we weren't attending. Although they had just walked past a whole ruckus of concrete gnomes and zoo animals, there wasn't a smile among them when Mimi let them in. My grandmother told them that she coughed too much, that she'd disrupt the service. "But think of the child," Mrs. Broward said, grabbing my upper arms and snatching me to my feet. "One day she'll have to stand before her Maker."

Mimi hung her head and said that since she'd be seeing God first, she'd take the blame. He'd understand. All she was trying to do was keep food on the table. She trailed them to the door. "He's a merciful God, isn't He?" The women said they hoped so, for our sakes, and marched back down the walk. The truth is, I wouldn't mind going back, but not if it meant giving up Sundays at the Show.

"Ten minutes, Rox, then I'm leaving without you."

"Coming!" I pulled my overalls on, shoved my feet into sneakers. I left my room, laces dragging, my pack hanging off one shoulder—then rushed back and buried the diary in my underwear drawer.

I was wolfing a piece of toast when it hit me. I stopped in mid-chew. My mother had borrowed Edison sources from someone named Lynda. All of a sudden, I knew who Lynda was. Lynda Smathers. The Smathers lived at the other end of our road. When I was really little, Lynda moved out to marry the Mr. Tully who owns the hardware store. She works for Forever Flowers in Crawfordville. She was the one who did the arrangements for Grandpa's funeral.

∼

I thought about it all day in class. Lynda Smathers—now Mrs. Tully—had known my mother. I didn't plan to do anything with the information, but then my cousin made a stop as he drove me home from school. "Got to get a flapper for the toilet," he said, and he pulled up in front of Tully's Hardware. In the strip mall across the lot were the Dollar General, Black's Automotive, and at the far end, with a pink awning over the door, Forever Flowers: Arrangements for All Occasions. I could see Mrs. Tully through the glass. I could almost hear Lucy telling me to go in. Okay, I told the Lucy in my head. I'll go in, but it doesn't mean I'll ask about my mother.

"I'm going in there," I said, pointing. My cousin didn't even look to see which of the stores in the strip I was pointing to; he just said to be quick. I told myself I'd get a flower for Mimi. But my stupid heart didn't believe me; it was trying to punch its way out of my chest. The bell jangled as I opened the door.

"Can I help you with something, hon?" Mrs. Tully, who stood behind the counter, picked up a rose and stripped off the lower leaves.

"I'm looking for Mrs. Tully," I said, even though I knew it was her.

She jabbed the rose stem into the foam block at the bottom of the vase she was filling and smiled. "Well, you found her." She picked up another rose. As she gave it a little shake to separate it from the others, the butterfly hair clips in her frizzy yellow hair batted their wings. Annarose had a pair just like them from the Dollar Store. "Say, you're Roxanne Piermont, aren't you?"

"Yes, ma'am."

"Haven't seen you since you quit coming to church. You've grown some. Well, Roxanne, what can I do you for?"

"Um, I'm just looking around while John Martin buys a flapper over at the hardware."

"I keep meaning to pop by to see your grandma. How is Miss Marilyn?"

"She's okay."

"I was real sorry to hear your granddaddy passed. The kids and I left for Disney the morning of the service or we would have been there."

"The flowers were nice." She was smiling at the compliment when I opened my mouth and the words just spilled out. "You were a friend of my mother's, weren't you?"

"Gracious. That was a long time ago. Back when we were both kids."

"But you *do* remember her, don't you?"

"A little. So much time has passed. We ran with different crowds." She turned to the glass case that held the buckets of flowers as if she needed something, but she didn't get anything out.

I rested my arms on the cool glass counter. "Could you tell me what you do remember? Was she pretty?"

"Pretty?" She turned back around and fussed with a hair clip—probably stalling while she thought of a polite way to say, no, she was a dog. Her answer was barely audible. "Yes, Ellie was pretty."

"You called her Ellie?"

"That's what we all called her."

"And she was… *pretty?* How pretty?"

"You must've seen a picture." She acted as if I was making fun of her.

"No ma'am, I haven't."

"Prettier than was good for her," she said, tapping her fingernails on the glass. "Not counting Laura Brandt, she was the prettiest girl in the class." She covered her mouth with her hand, hiding a smile. "Except for that time when she plucked all her eyebrows out."

"She plucked them *all* out?"

"Uh-huh. It made her look all wide-open and surprised."

"What was my mother like?" I asked quickly. "Her personality, I mean." But Mrs. Tully was watching something out the window. When I turned, I saw John Martin and her husband standing on the sidewalk by the wheelbarrows. As he threw his head back to laugh, Mr. Tully's big round glasses winked in the sunlight. He slapped my cousin's back. They might be a while—Mimi liked to say that Mr. Tully could talk the hind leg off the Lamb of God—but I couldn't count on it.

"Please," I rushed on. "What was my mother like?"

"Ellie was always...restless." She twisted the ring on her finger. "Always wishing for things she couldn't have." She stared at the fleck of diamond in its heart-shaped setting and pressed her lips together.

"What kinds of things?"

"Oh, I don't know. Nice things. Things that belonged to other people." Her eyes went back to the men in front of the hardware store. "Ellie wanted to be going somewhere and doing something every minute, even if it was just riding up and down Crawfordville Highway." She snapped another rose stem with the clippers and nodded toward the window. "Looks like their little powwow's breaking up. Your cousin'll be looking for you, hon."

John Martin was shaking hands with Mr. Tully. They must have been on their nine millionth handshake, but Mr. Tully hung on, still talking, still laughing.

John Martin looked toward the line of stores, hunting for me.

"Just tell me one more thing," I said quickly. I wasn't in trouble as long as Mr. Tully had my cousin fly-papered in front of the hardware store. "Do I look like her?"

"Look like her? Well, let me see..." She took a pair of glasses out of the pocket of her smock. "Your hair color's kinda close."

I could tell she wasn't seeing anything of Ellie, the second prettiest girl in school, in me. "Maybe I look like my father," I blurted out, although I had never mentioned my father to anyone but Mimi, ever.

The gauzy wings of the butterflies on her clips trembled. "I wouldn't know about that," she whispered. "Looks like you better scoot. Remember me to Miss Marilyn, okay?" and she disappeared through a door between the flower coolers.

"Thank you, Mrs. Tully," I called after her, wondering what spooked her. "I'll do that." I had picked up a couple more things for my list. **Restless** and **Pretty.** It wasn't exactly news that Joelle's mother, Laura Brandt, would be prettier than mine. The surprise was that my mother was pretty too. Maybe I was what Mimi called a late bloomer. Maybe I'd grow up okay looking after all.

I left the store grinning and singing to myself, *my mother was pretty, my mother was pretty,* over and over like some dumb nursery rhyme. The door had hardly closed behind me when a voice boomed across the parking lot. "Roxy!" It was Mr. Tully. "Come on inside and pick yourself out some candy."

John Martin patted his shirt pocket. "I already have the two mints."

"Didn't want to hurt your feelings, John, but she's a fireball girl these days, aren't ya, Roxy?"

"How'd you remember that, Mr. Tully?" I asked.

"'Cause you're my girl!" Mr. Tully had three boys, but he must've wanted a girl bad. He was always so nice to me. Now he clapped a hand on my back and guided me into the dark interior of the store. Mr. Tully is even bigger than John Martin. He's tall, but thin, with a long friendly face like a hound. And he's nice. I knew the way perfectly, but he guided me along aisles where the wooden floor was worn into shallow troughs. We passed the carousels of seed packets and bins of loose seed John Martin and I spend hours in front of every spring and fall.

With a clang and a flourish, Mr. Tully lifted the lid of the jar on the counter. I fished out two fireballs. "Thanks, Mr. Tully."

When we got in the truck my cousin took the two wrapped mints out of his pocket and tossed them on the dashboard with the half dozen other hard candies already rattling around up there. I untwirled the cellophane on one of the fireballs and popped it in my mouth. I was afraid John Martin was going to ask why I went to the florist's. Instead he said, "You oughta lay off the candy, Rox. All this sugar can't be good for you."

"What do you want me to do, spit it out?" I sucked on the peppery candy, still sing-songing *my mother was pretty* inside my head.

Chapter 10
The Absolute Cutest

Don't tell me you never made fried chicken before," Mimi said, pulling two chickens out of a plastic bag. "Didn't your mother teach you anything?"

"She taught me French and how to get stains off silk." Lucy stuffed her hands in the back pockets of her jeans. "She taught me how to do the fox-trot."

"You should teach John Martin that fox-trot thing some time," I said, poking him under the table with my sock foot. "You like to dance, don't you, John Martin?" Above the table he ignored me; below he kicked my shin.

Mimi held up a rubbery bird. "Okay," she said. "We'll start basic. Lucy, this is a chicken. It's raw, and we're gonna cook it." She hooked a finger inside and yanked out a white paper package, which she tore open over a saucepan. Out spilled the purple liver, the stringy gizzard, the nubbly neck.

Lucy gawked. "What are *those?*"

"Spare parts," I said. "Milton gets the gizzard." I didn't want Lucy to think we were the kind of people who would eat those little bags of grit.

"The rest of it goes into my famous giblet gravy," Mimi said.

Gravy? I mouthed at John Martin. It had been ages since Mimi made gravy.

Mimi whacked the chickens in pieces with a big knife, showing Lucy where the joints were. While she mixed up batter she had Lucy slice and bread okra. Then my grandmother whumped a pair of black skillets onto the stove and began spooning Crisco into them.

"Isn't that a lot of fat?" Lucy asked.

"It don't sink in." Mimi struck a match and lit the burners, then a cigarette, and tossed the match in the sink. The fat in the pans had just begun to pop when Mimi pushed up her sleeves and set the cigarette on the edge of the stove. "Stand back," she told Lucy. "I need me some elbow room." We hadn't seen her cook like that since Grandpa Bill died. It was like having the old Mimi back. Even John Martin quit studying to watch her.

≈

Powder biscuits and creamed corn. Fried okra and chicken, with sweet pickles in a glass dish. We sat down to a dinner like the old days. "If only your Grandpa was here," Mimi said. She took a bite and made a face. "The chicken might could use a little more salt." But of course it was perfect.

Everything was perfect. Plus with Lucy there, we were four at the table again. The exact right number.

I didn't think about the diary until I climbed into bed. Then I got up again and dug it out of the drawer along with the flashlight. Flashlight tucked against the side of my neck, I shined the beam on the page. The date at the top, January 4, had been replaced with January 16. Helen was slacking off even faster than I had in my diary.

January 16
Dear Diary,

Lynda sez I stole her stupid purple pen. All I did was <u>borrow</u> it cause I didn't have one for the test. I didn't think I had to ask my best friend. When she said I sniched it I couldn't say well here *it is thank you for the lone. Someday when she's out I'll sneak it in her purse. Then won't she feel bad for saying I took it. I probly failed the test anyway. Ma's gonna ground me til I'm 53.*

—Miss Understood (get it?)

The writing was purple. I flipped the pages, not reading, just looking at the ink. Purple, purple, purple. Then light purple, then lavender. With each page it got fainter, like footprints walking away from the edge of the water. The lavender vanished in the middle of the page, in the middle of a word. After that the ink was blue. I wondered who she stole that pen from.

I added **Steals things** to my list, then crossed it out and wrote, **Borrows.** But something else was bothering me. Mrs. Tully had said that she and my mother ran with different crowds, but according to the diary they were best friends. So I wrote **Best Friend—Lynda Smathers???**

February 12
Dear Diary,

Pop says I have to ware my church dress to the Valentines party! My church shoes 2! According to him if there good enuff for the Lord there good enuff to go hopping around with a bunch of kids in the gym. Ma wants to give me a perm but I don't know. She has no fashun sense when it comes to hair. If she messes up it will never grow out to my waste. Of course Lynda has a new dress—not that it helps. A pig in a dress is still a pig. Ma sez I have to wash all the windas in the house if I want to go at all.

—Cinderella

I winced when I read about the pig in a dress. That's what I felt like when I put one on. That's why I wear overalls. They cover all the piggy parts.

February 14
Dear Diary,

Just back from the dance. I didn't let Ma perm me. Lynda gave me a hair cundishuner sample out of one of her moms magazines. I wore my hair loose. At least it hid the stupid colar on my church dress. I borrowed Ma's lipstick and put it on in the girls room.

Lynda looked like a stuffed satin candy box in her new dress. Chet asked her to dance 2 times then she stepped on his foot. I took off my church shoes and danced in my stockings. She held my purse.

DIARY—THIS IS THE BEST PART. Robbie stayed home with a bad cold but Jack asked me to dance 4 times! He is the absaloot cutest!!!! My dress still smells like his colone. I don't want to wash it ever!!!

—Helen

I wrote **Likes exclamation points**, but something else was on my mind. I looked at the last entry on my list: **Best Friend—Lynda Smathers???** So far she'd called her best friend a pig and a candy box. I didn't feel so great about her being pretty any more, not if it made her act like Joelle McBride. I added **Tends to be critical.** It was better than writing **Disloyal** or **Mean.**

I put the diary under my pillow and switched off the flashlight. I could hear John Martin and Lucy horsing around downstairs. I wished I was down there with them, the diary still buried in my drawer. I tried to be glad Helen got to dance with the absolute cutest guy. If it was me that would mean dancing with George Daniel—like that could happen. If I had been there, I would have been Lynda, stepping on Chet's feet and looking like a stuffed satin candy box.

Chapter 11
The Wizard of
Menlo Park

C an I turn?" Annarose whispered.
"Turn what?" I asked.
"The page. Are you done reading it?"
"Sure, go ahead." Annarose and I were sharing an Edison book at a table in the media center. Neither of us would touch a book about him ever again. The Edison report cured Wakulla County kids of interest in the lightbulb forever. But even though this was the one time in my life I should have been interested, my mind wasn't on the famous inventor.

"Shouldn't you be taking notes?" Annarose whispered. She had already covered half a dozen cards with miniscule printing without taking a single note on his successful inventions. She'd overlooked the lightbulb, but had written down every detail of the time he wired the tails of two cats together and rubbed them to test the power of static electricity. Annarose's note concluded, *Edison might be smart, but he was also mean.*

I figured one of us should be taking notes on the experiments that actually worked, so I did my best to get interested in Thomas Alva Edison, inventor of electrical and communication devices including the incandescent lamp, the phonograph, and the microphone. Instead I pictured my mother in the gym, dancing with George Daniel. Since I didn't know what her class's cutest guy, Jack, looked like, I substituted ours. But no matter how hard I tried to imagine her, Helen looked like a brown-haired Joelle.

Annarose scribbled, then pushed a file card under my nose. *What are you thinking about?*

I wrote *Thomas Alva, who else?* and pushed it back at her.

Hah! wrote Annarose.

When it came time to check out books, Mrs. Canaday, the media specialist, rationed titles. With every kid in seventh doing a report, there was a serious Edison shortage. Annarose and I got *Edison: Wizard of Menlo Park,* copyright 1953.

"Hey, Annarose," I said. "Call your mom and see if you can come home with me to study."

Normally Mrs. Sneed doesn't like to drive out our way to get her; it's pretty far. Edison was a great excuse. So for once I had someone to sit with on the bus besides Mikey—who got really mad when Annarose took his spot. Mikey sat right behind us, breathing on our necks, trying to get one of us to play Hangman. When he threatened to cry, Annarose got out a pencil and paper. He hung her three times before the bus stopped at the top of my road. "You're way more fun than Rox," he yelled as we climbed off.

When we got in the house, I stuck my head in the living room. "I'm home, Mimi. Annarose too. We're working on Edison."

"Annarose?" Mimi called. She was watching Judge Judy on TV, but switched it off. "Come in and visit a minute, hon."

"I'm trying to!" Annarose yelled. "Rox, help!"

Milton had her flattened against the wall. I threw my arms around his chest and shouted, "Go!" While he pawed the air, she made a break for the living room.

"Annarose..." I could hear the pleasure in Mimi's voice as I got the three of us sodas.

"Hi, Mrs. Piermont. You look a little tired, are you feeling okay?"

"I *am* a little tired. Thanks for noticing."

Annarose is always noticing; that's why adults like her.

I could hear Mimi and my friend talking as the soda glugged out of the bottle. Annarose's part sounded like this: "No…how terrible for you…that must really hurt!"

Annarose's particular gift is caring—caring in the extreme. Sometimes it backfires, like the time I mentioned that Joelle was not looking like her usual stuck-up self. A little later Annarose dragged me to the girls' room, all woggle-eyed. "Guess what?" she said. "Joelle's daddy moved out of their house." Her lips trembled. "Isn't that sad!" Annarose went on to paint such a sad picture of poor old snooty Joelle missing her daddy I actually felt bad. Then, come to find out, her dad hadn't moved out at all. He had moved his *mom* out, to a nursing home. Annarose didn't miss a beat. She instantly switched to feeling sorry for the old lady.

"How awful for you!" Annarose was still going strong when I carried the clinking glasses of soda to the living room.

"Mimi," I said. "It's stuffy in here. And hot. I'll open a window."

"Don't, Rox. I've got a little chill." And she went back to showing off her symptoms to our visitor. "It's a twinge combined with burning," she said, lifting the blanket off her lap to point at her side. "A burny twinge. It wakes me up nights."

"Poor you!" gushed Annarose, the Niagara Falls of sympathy.

My friend and I drank our sodas and sweated. Mimi pulled the blanket up to her chin and said, "When the humidity is high, like now, it's like there's an elephant on my chest." I watched her talk, and even though she was animated by Annarose's visit, she looked tired, and every couple of sentences she stopped to cough. Judging by the way my friend looked at her, it was a miracle Mimi was still alive.

Seeing the concern on Annarose's face, I began to wonder if maybe all the twinges and burning and coughing added up to something serious. I didn't want to think about it. "We need to work on Edison," I announced.

"Edison?" they repeated together.

"The wizard of Menlo Park, remember?"

Mimi waved a hand. "Don't let me keep you two from your schoolwork."

Annarose stood and pulled her skirt away from her sweaty legs. "A pleasure talking to you, Mrs. Piermont."

"The same," said Mimi, burrowing under the blanket and closing her eyes. "Come again when you're not doing Edison." Annarose promised that she would.

We dropped our packs on the floor of my room. "Down," I said, as Milton climbed onto the bed.

"Let him stay," begged Annarose. "He's getting old and the floor is so hard."

"I don't think the bed can take all three of us." But we all piled on. When nothing broke she took out her file cards.

"I'm sorry we can't spread these out on the desk," I said. Like Mimi with her garden sculptures, I collect. My specialty is animals made of china or glass, the smaller the better. Still, small adds up. We couldn't even see the desktop.

We smoothed the wrinkles in the bedspread and laid out the cards. I flopped down on my stomach and reached into my pack to retrieve *Edison: Wizard of Menlo Park*. "Okay, where were we?"

She consulted her notes. "The last thing I wrote down was his nickname when he worked for the telegraph company. They called him the Loony. Here, give me the book. I can find it." She was flipping through the pages when something caught her eye. "Now, why would anyone do that?" She plopped the open book down in front of me. Someone with a purple pen had drawn mustaches on Edison's second wife, Mina Miller, and the three Edison children—Madeleine, Charles, and Theodore. Thomas Alva, whose bare upper lip could have used one, was mustache-free, but he had a purple arrow sticking out either side of his head. *Why didn't you dye young, Thomas A?* was scrawled across the front of his white shirt.

"What's wrong?" Annarose asked.

How could she tell that something was wrong? All I did was breathe in. "I think that's my mother's handwriting," I said.

She gasped. "Your mother put mustaches on the Edisons?"

I nodded. "At least I think so."

Already huge behind thick glasses, her eyes got bigger. "What makes you think it was her?" Except for what I'd learned in the diary she knew everything I did about my mother. Which was basically nothing except for the fact that she was gone.

"Trust me," I said. "It was her. I just know."

"But how?" she pressed.

"I'll tell you, but only if you swear, I mean *swear* you won't tell anyone—not even your mom." Annarose told her mother everything.

"I swear," she whispered. "Not even my mom."

I got the diary out of my drawer.

"What's that?"

"Her diary. Lucy and I found it in the attic." I opened it to *Helen May Piermont. This is her book, 1986.*

"Wow," she breathed.

I let her read as far as I had. I know I should have shared with Lucy first, but Lucy would want to read the whole thing right away and blab to John Martin about it. Annarose was much more obedient, and she never ever lied. If she promised not to tell she wouldn't.

Every now and then my friend would glance at the handwriting on Thomas Alva's chest. "It looks kind of similar, but you shouldn't jump to any conclusions." But *she* jumped when she reached the page in the diary where the ink turned purple.

"See what I mean?" I asked. "It's the same, right?"

"Well, it sure looks like it."

She read everything up to February 14, and handed the diary back. "Wow," she said again.

I sprawled back against Milton. "What do you think of her?"

"She sounds...fun."

"Does she sound like someone we would have as a friend?"

"Us?" Annarose patted Milton, stirring up a flurry of loose hair. She shrugged her round shoulders. "I don't know. She sounds pretty popular. Like at that dance? That would never happen to us." I knew she was remembering a dance the two of us went to together in the sixth grade. We didn't dance at all. Charles got both of us punch, then the three of us sat on the floor, our backs against the wall. "Do you think she'd have us for friends?" she asked.

"Not unless we wanted to hold her purse." We laughed, but it was like we were laughing at ourselves.

"I know *I* wouldn't like her." As soon as I said it I swallowed hard. Had I just said that I didn't like my mother? I hadn't even let myself *think* it before.

I saw the shock in Annarose's blue eyes. "Rox, she's your mother…"

Too late to take it back. I pushed ahead. "Big deal. She sounds mean and stuck up. It's like reading Joelle's diary, only Joelle spells better."

"Now, Rox, you don't know she's mean and stuck up. You haven't read the whole thing."

"Right, she might turn out to be a saint."

"Right!" Annarose echoed with a big smile. "She might."

"I was kidding, Annarose." Annarose doesn't recognize sarcasm. It's one of her shortcomings.

"But maybe it's true," she insisted. "Maybe on the very next page she shows her good side."

"The next page?" I doubted it, but I wanted to be wrong. I opened the diary to the next page and read aloud.

March 3
Dear Diary,

I hate hate hate him!!! Spud is such a pain. All I did was role my skirt up at the waste while we were waiting for the bus. No one but Lynda wears a skirt halfway to there ankles. I told him not to tell. He said he woodn't so of course he did. He said he had his fingers crossed when he promised.

Why couldn't I have a different family with a sister to share

93

*clothes and a pretty house with a real paved road in front of it?
Why is my life ruined every time I turn around? I hate hate hate
all three of them.*

—*Going Crazy Helen*

Annarose was silent. Helen had punched the sympathy out of her with all those *hates*. For a moment Annarose teetered like a sailboat about to flip, then she righted herself. "She must have been *desperately* unhappy," she whispered, her magnified eyes beginning to look shiny.

Outside, someone tapped a car horn. "Shoot! It's my mom!" she said. "And we haven't done a thing about Edison." Aside from thirty minutes of admiring Mimi's symptoms, we had spent all our time on Helen May Piermont, book vandal of Wakulla County.

"Here, take the book with you," I told her. "You take better notes." Even if they're weird, I added to myself.

As Annarose stuffed Edison in her pack she giggled. "Say hi to *Spud* for me!" Mrs. Sneed leaned on the car horn and she jumped up. "See ya tomorrow, Rox." And she thundered down the stairs.

I closed the diary and tried to think like Annarose. My mother was unhappy, maybe even desperately. She had a pesty cousin making her life miserable. Her skirts were too long. I felt a twitch of sympathy and did my best to encourage it.

Then I remembered she hated her family. *My* family. She would have gladly traded Mimi and Grandpa Bill and John Martin for a sister with pretty clothes and a paved road. My sympathy shriveled like a dried pea.

I considered burning the diary, or taking it to school and stuffing it in the cafeteria trash with the half cartons of milk and the baloney sandwiches. I was fed up with Helen May Piermont. I didn't like her. I had been happier when everything I knew about her fit in a shoe box. In the end I buried her at the bottom of my underwear drawer again. She could just sit in there a while.

Chapter 12
Girls' Night Out

I didn't learn much about Edison for the next couple of days. Annarose left the book home on Thursday. Friday night I had it, but Lucy had a better idea than working on Edison. "Mrs. Piermont, Rox, let's go see a movie. Girls' night out, my treat. If we hustle we can make the eight-thirty show."

Mimi had already collapsed in Grandpa Bill's recliner. Feet up, she was watching TV over the toes of his old slippers. "Some other time, maybe. I'm pooped," she said.

"Please, Mimi," I begged. "Please!"

"I'll just get your sweater, Mrs. Piermont." Lucy marched into the kitchen to retrieve it off the back of a chair.

John Martin was studying at the kitchen table. "Give it up, Luce," I heard him say. "You'd have to hire a crane to pry her out once she's in that chair. And she shouldn't be running around anyway. She's been sick."

I leaned over the back of the recliner and draped my arms around Mimi's neck. "Are you going to let him tell you what you should do?" I whispered.

Lucy came back into the living room holding out Mimi's sweater. "Come on." She swished it a couple of times, making it dance. "Put your arms in the sleeves."

"What are we seeing?" Mimi eyed the sweater suspiciously. "Not blood and guts, I hope." She shoved an arm into a sleeve. "I hate blood and guts." She leaned forward so Lucy could slide the sweater behind her back.

"Stuff some tissues in your pocket," said Lucy, guiding Mimi's hand into the second sleeve. "We're going to a chick flick. Hey, Johnny!" she shouted. "Quit thinking calculus a minute and put Mrs. Piermont's chair in the pickup. Toss me the keys while you're at it."

I tugged the handle on the lounge chair, catapulting Mimi to her feet. Lucy tried to take her by the elbow and hustle her to the door, but Mimi wouldn't budge.

"If I'm going to town I need to put my face on and find some shoes."

"Please, Mimi," I said. "Not the face." The movie started in less than an hour. "It'll be dark in the theater."

"I'll do the quick version," she assured us.

I got behind her and pushed her up the stairs. She can get there by herself, but we didn't have all night. We were going to the movies!

~

Mimi huffed back down the stairs. "That didn't take long, did it?"

"No time at all," Lucy agreed.

"A new record," I said. Lucy and I each took an arm and led Mimi out to the truck. I was scared to take a closer look at my grandmother's speed-record face. In a glance I'd seen the penciled eyebrows that flew like birds across her forehead, the lumpy mascara and turquoise eyelids. Her red lipstick had missed most of her mouth. She reeked of gardenia perfume and hair spray. But at least she was ready.

We helped her up into the truck. Lucy got behind the wheel. I was squeezed between them, the shift chucking me in the knee.

"Is this all the faster you can go?" Mimi asked. "You're as poky as John Martin." She clutched her giant black purse as Lucy pushed the pedal to the floor and our shoulder blades dug into the seat. "Well," she said, "that's more like it."

Lucy parked as close to the entrance as she could, then the two of us struggled to lower the wheelchair from the back of the pickup. By the time we guided Mimi into the darkened theater the good seats were all taken, the credits rolling. We had to sit near the front at the end of a row with Mimi parked in the aisle. "Too bad we missed all the previews," hissed Mimi, like a trip to the movies wasn't a once-a-millennium thing for us.

We shared a bucket of popcorn. Mimi complained it'd get under her dentures, then ate a bunch anyway.

On screen, the kissing started. From our close-up angle, the stars' lips were huge. Mimi covered my eyes with a buttery hand when the tongue-wrestling began. "You're too young for this part," she whispered.

"And you're too old," I whispered back, sliding away from the hand.

After a while the movie got sad. Mimi dredged a wad of tissues out of her purse and passed them out to Lucy and me. "Here, hon," she said, poking the woman in the row ahead of us. "You want a hankie?" The woman took one and blew hard.

"That Nic Cage," said Mimi on the way home. "He's not much to look at, but he has such sensitive eyes." She honked her nose, then stuffed the tissue up the sleeve of her sweater and heaved a shuddery sigh. "It was *so* romantic."

John Martin was waiting at the window. "You're back," he said as he came out the door. He leaped from the porch to the ground. "How are you, Ma? I was beginning to worry."

"Oh, you worry too much." She took his arm and he helped her out of the truck. "We had a good time. I ate popcorn—can't wait to get my dentures out. But the movie was great. I had myself a good old cry."

Seated at the kitchen table, she told him the whole movie.

Between crying and eating, her makeup had spread until it looked as if her face had been used as a target in a paint-ball war. But no one laughed, or even smiled. Mimi was so excited. "The only bad thing," she concluded, "was we missed the previews."

"Next time, Ma." John Martin put an arm around her waist and eased her out of the chair. "Now, off to bed. You and Rox have the Show to do in the morning."

"You're a bad influence, Lucy," Mimi shouted over her shoulder as he walked her out of the kitchen. "I won't be worth spit in the morning, thanks to you. You have no respect for your elders."

"You're welcome, Mrs. Piermont," Lucy shouted back. We could hear their feet on the steps.

Mimi must have stopped in the hall before John Martin could steer her into her bedroom. "You have plans for next Friday night, Lucy Everhart?" she yelled.

"Not really." Lucy winked at me across the table. "You have any, Mrs. Piermont?"

"Sure. Girls' night out."

Chapter 13
The Smell of Trouble

W hy did you two let her talk me into it?" Mimi groaned. "I feel like I been run over by a truck. Check my back for tire marks, Rox." She took the spoon out of the sugar bowl and tipped the bowl over her morning coffee. Sugar poured like sand off a dump truck.

John Martin drummed his fingers on the table. "You mind chugging that coffee, Ma? We're running late."

"I still need to do my war paint." Mimi had hogged the bathroom for a good half hour, swabbing last night's makeup off with cold cream, but she hadn't put on today's face yet. She took a sip of her coffee and grimaced. "It's cold."

My cousin walked her cup to the microwave, his heavy work boots impatient on the worn linoleum. "I been late the last couple of Saturdays, Ma, and the schedule's tight. We're hanging Sheetrock. Painters come first thing tomorrow, so we have to finish up today, no ifs or buts."

The oven beeped and John Martin handed the coffee to Mimi, who took a teeny sip. "Too hot," she said, pushing the cup away. "Don't let me hold you up. The world will have to take me as is."

"Let me at least get your lipstick," I said. As I dashed upstairs I thought, this isn't like Mimi. She never goes anywhere without her face.

I slid the cap off and handed her the lipstick. I held up a mirror. She took a couple of general swipes at her lips and gave the lipstick

back. "You can't go like that," I said. "You look like you're smirking."
I picked up a tissue and wiped off the splotch under her lower lip.
"Want to comb your hair?"

"Not particularly."

"All right then!" John Martin dumped her coffee down the sink.
"Let's go." John Martin didn't see a thing wrong with Mimi going
out wearing a sinister smirk of lipstick, her hair blasting straight out
like a blowtorch. The symptoms he worried about were things like
tingling and numbness, the cough that never went away. But to me,
Mimi going out without her face was scarier. It was like she was losing track of herself.

~

"Go see Marie," I ordered, turning a pumpkin so the side that had
rested in the dirt faced away from the public.

Mimi stared at her own hands. "Maybe later."

"Want your crochet?"

"No, I don't want that heavy old thing on my lap. I'll just sit." She
picked up a fan from the junk on the table. "The air feels awful close
today, don't you think, Rox? This is the hottest October I can
remember."

"You just forget," I told her. "It hardly ever gets cold before
Christmas." I pulled my shirt away from my skin. When no one was
looking, I sniffed a pit to make sure my deodorant was working.

I lifted one of the wreaths I had piled in a grocery bag. "How
much for these?"

She barely gave the wreath a glance. "I don't know. How about five?"

"What about the twenty-five we talked about when we were making them?"

"Talk is cheap. We might could go seven."

"Remember the way we cut our hands on the cones? Remember
how it took John Martin and me two whole afternoons to gather
them in the first place?"

"Put whatever price you want." She waved the fan. "It don't matter to me."

"I'll put nine. That way the customer'll get change back from a ten. There's plenty of time to mark them down before Christmas."

"Christmas," Mimi sighed. "It just isn't the same since your grandpa died. He sure did love the holidays."

During the holidays Grandpa Bill used to sit in his recliner, eyeglasses blinking red and green from the Christmas tree lights. He would smoke or read the paper, the same things he did any other time of year.

"You know," Mimi said, studying the chipped polish on her nails, "when he was young your grandfather looked a little like that Nic Cage. Just as skinny with those droopy, sheepdog eyes. And handsome? Well, you've seen the wedding pictures."

The flashbulb had caught my grandfather looking surprised in a coat and tie; that was probably the only time in his life he wore a suit and didn't go to a funeral. He had a big nose and big ears, and he must've been standing on a box to make himself taller than the plump young bride hanging off his arm. He didn't look a bit like a movie star and he wasn't handsome. Except to Mimi.

Her eyes got misty. "When they made Bill Piermont they broke the mold. They surely did."

"Did Nic Cage do this to you?" I demanded.

She lifted a hand, empty palm up. A tear slithered down her cheek.

I threw my arms around her neck, "You have me, Mimi. You have John Martin." My fingers had glitter on them from the wreaths. I rubbed a couple of sparkles on her tired old arm. "Magic fairy dust," I said, but the magic didn't work. She seemed to be shrinking as she sat in her chair, Mimi who was usually so tough. I didn't know what to do.

"Marilyn! Thank God you're okay!" Spice Marie was barreling toward us. "You were sick last week, and then when you didn't show up for our usual little chat today...I got worried." She stopped and

101

looked at Mimi's freaky hair and twist-o lipstick. "You're a living fright, Marilyn. You come with me to the Ladies' before you scare off all the customers." The two of them moved slowly, Mimi's chair whirring, Marie's hand on her shoulder. "Listen," Marie said as they passed the Gonzalez's stand, "Ferry Morgan's selling goldfish today. Be good and I'll get you a couple."

When Mimi came back from a long visit with Marie, her hair was on straight, her lips were in the right place, and a plastic bag holding three goldfish was swinging off the back of her chair.

She took one look at our wreaths priced at nine dollars and pitched a fit. "Mercy me, why don't you just *give* them away, Rox! They should be twelve, at least."

~

It didn't take long to realize that the bottom had fallen out of the pumpkin market. Ditto pipe-cleaner spiders. Most folks said they already had their jack-'o-lanterns, and those who didn't must have figured out that in four days, when trick-or-treat was over, all they'd have was a rotting squash on their front steps.

By ten I had taken all the spiders out of my hair—I'd have to find another use for black pipe cleaners. By ten-thirty I'd sold the last bunch of Indian corn. I began humming Christmas carols.

"Stop it," Mimi complained. "It's too hot for carols." There were rings of sweat under her arms. Since returning from Marie's makeover, Mimi had been sliding toward gloom again. She reached back and took the bag of fish off the handle of the chair and watched them swim. "What do I do with these? We don't have a tank and they're too small to fry."

The breeze felt as hot and wet as Milton's breath.

"Be a doll, Rox, and get me another sweet tea from the concession. *Three* cubes."

I sold my first wreath at eleven-thirty—a hard sell. "It doesn't have a hanger on the back," the woman whined. "How am I supposed to hang it without a hanger?" I turned a black pipe cleaner into a wreath hanger. Then she wanted to give me ten for it, but I told her that this wreath was unique, a local craft that she wouldn't find in any old store. She paid the twelve dollars, but she didn't walk away happy.

~

Jerome was the first to notice. He was getting something out of his van when I saw him frown. "Sky looks funny, Tire King," he called.

Danny stepped out from under the shed roof and looked too. "I don't see nothing different. Sky looks kinda dull, maybe."

Jerome wrinkled his nose and tapped it with one finger. "Something big coming," he said. "I smell it."

Danny inhaled deeply. "What's it smell like?"

"Like trouble, man."

"Trouble?" Danny walked around, nose in the air, trying to catch a whiff of trouble, but the smell of Goodyear rubber was in his shirt and jeans, probably even his skin; he couldn't get away from it.

Stacking his paintings front to back so the velvet wouldn't rub, Jerome began to pack.

"Hey, what're you doing?" Danny asked. "You already paid for the day."

"Tomorrow," said Jerome, loading the first pile in his van. "Maybe. The world is out of balance."

Mr. Gonzalez was putting mangoes in a bag. He looked up as Jerome drove away. Danny touched the side of the head and Mr. Gonzalez nodded; just crazy Jerome, they both thought.

I walked out our side of the shed and away from the smell of tires and pinecones and piled fruit. I took a deep breath. The wind smelled like metal. There was a strange taste at the back of my tongue. From that side of the market, I had a clear view of a part of the sky Danny and Jerome had been unable to see. It was dull and dark and colored like a bruise.

Something coming, I thought.

103

"What do you think is going to happen?" I asked Mimi, who was making change for one of the last people on earth who hadn't gotten word that it was too late to buy a pumpkin.

"Come see us again," she said, then turned to me. "What do you mean, happen?"

"I don't know. Jerome said—"

"Jerome always says. He's full of voodoo and chicken hearts and black magic." She rolled her chair to the edge of the slab to study the sky. "I say it's going to rain like heck. Better sell what we can, while we can. Stick a half-price sign on those pumpkins, Rox."

I made the sign, then did my best to concentrate on the customers. Humming "Silent Night," I put another wreath in a bag.

As usual, Danny's business ran hot and cold. Sometimes he was rolling out tires like a circus performer with a weird juggling act. But most of the time he sat on the tailgate of his truck, smoked, and swung his legs. After Jerome left, he alternated sitting and walking out to look at the sky. Each time he inhaled deeply, as if he was trying to catch the scent of trouble. I was selling gourds to Mrs. Burdick—one of my regulars—when I saw Danny shade his eyes and stare. "Hey, Carlos," he called. "Come take a look."

Mr. Gonzalez joined him. "Holy Mary, Mother of God," said Mr. Gonzalez, which was more English than I thought he knew.

"What's the matter, boys?" Mimi teased. "Afraid of a little rain?"

But the men just stood there, hands hanging, eyes on the clouds.

Danny spat over his shoulder. "What do you say, Carlos? Do we pack it in?"

Mr. Gonzalez gazed across the shed to the heaps of fruits and vegetables. He had lost business to rain the week before and gone home with his truck half full.

Danny eyed the mounds of tires. Tires are easy to drop from the back of a truck, but hard work to reload. Instead of making a decision, Danny shook a couple of cigarettes out his pack and offered one to Mr. Gonzalez. They smoked and watched the sky.

Mimi sold a half-price pumpkin. "We're having a great day, Rox!"

I wanted to check the sky again to see if the trouble was moving toward us or away, but we were surrounded. Customers, two deep, pawed through the junk. I sold a set of nesting Corning Ware bowls and a potato masher. First break I got, I dashed out into the vendor's lot and took another look.

The sky sagged. In the distance behind the last of the three long sheds that housed the flea market, the cloud curtain flickered with lightning. A few gray tufts hung like the twisted threads at the edge of a pair of old cutoffs. Across the lot in the second wing of the market I saw Ferry Morgan. "What are those, Mr. Morgan?" I yelled.

"What are what, Rox?" He stepped out and walked toward me.

"Those things hanging off the clouds."

Mr. Morgan turned, hitched his pants up, and whistled between his teeth. "Tornadoes. Lucky thing they're up high. Better hope they don't touch down."

I woke up Marco, who was sleeping under the Gonzalez's table. I didn't know how much English his parents understood. I took him out and showed him the tufts hanging down from the clouds. He showed his father. "He says we should wait and see," said Marco, crawling back under the table.

Mimi called me over to help a woman who wanted to buy an egg slicer. I was putting it in a bag when I saw Charles Ames stumbling down the aisle between displays. He almost knocked an old lady down, but didn't stop. When he got to the bench in front of our table he climbed up on it. "Listen, everybody. Listen." He waved his arms. "We're under a tornado warning. *Warning,* not watch. Y'all better go."

"Do we have time to pack up?" Danny asked.

Charles put his hands on his thighs, winded from running. He shook his head, no, then half-jumped, half-fell off the bench and took off for his home booth.

There was an uneasy silence. Everyone ducked to see a little more of the sky below the edge of the roof. One customer picked up her daughter, who was really too tall to carry, and ran with her in her arms. The girl's sneakers swung, striking the woman's knees, but she kept on running. I watched them until they cut between Mrs. Yu and Mack's Boiled Peanuts. When I looked back at the area around our table, the only customer left was a guy buying a cup and saucer from Mimi. "Keep the change," he said, and hurried away.

After that it was only vendors. Vendors and stuff. And no one wanted to leave their stuff behind. Mr. Gonzalez waved his arms. *"Vamanos!"* And the rest of his family crowded into the cab of the truck. He had his key out, ready to drive away, but he stopped. The mangoes and avocados glistened in their boxes. He kissed the cross that hung around his neck and began heaving crates of vegetables into the back.

Danny took a long look at his piles of tires, and went over to help Mr. Gonzalez.

The only thing I could think to do was put our stuff under the table. I moved the perfume bottles, the stacks of china, the ugly beer stein. I crawled around, pushing everything together. I could see Ferry Morgan loading his truck. Chickens scolded as he slung their cages into the back. Feathers flashed. Mr. Morgan usually moved them gently and called them ladies. Now he was tossing them around like pillows in a pillow fight.

The wind thrashed the party dresses on the rack over Mrs. Yu's head. As she climbed up on a chair and dragged down an armload, the gauzy fabric wound itself around her like a cocoon. She walked blindly toward the open trunk of her rusted Cadillac. From all around, I heard the sounds of engines starting, the slam of vehicle doors.

"Mimi, what should we do?" I asked. We had no way to leave.

"Nothing. Everybody's gone loony. Tornado! Not a thing in this world is going to happen, and—"

"Here she comes!" Ferry Morgan had walked out to the middle of the parking lot and started hollering, as loud as any of his roosters. He started toward the big cages, which held goats and a heifer, then slapped his hand on top of his Stetson and ran for his truck.

When I looked back everyone was running. "This way, Mimi," I shouted. While most of the market was nothing more than tin roofs on poles, the concession stands built on either side of the walkway were concrete block. We had to get inside one of them.

I ran a few feet before I realized she wasn't with me. "Mimi?"

She was fiddling with the controls on her chair. "Go on, Rox, I'll catch up."

I ran back and grabbed the wheelchair's handles. I pushed. "The brake, Mimi!"

She fumbled with the brake. It was like a nightmare; a monster was coming and we couldn't get out of its way. Suddenly, the brake sprang loose and I fell forward. I had to sprint to keep up with the chair. As I ran I heard a low sound, like the warning growl of a dog. Behind us Miss Louise wailed, "Help me, somebody, help me up! Don't leave me here!"

Sorry, sorry, I can't help you, Miss Louise. The thought trailed me like a string. But you're too heavy for a tornado to lift, Miss Louise. You're a rock; you're a mountain. Your weight will save you. I wanted to believe it because I was running away when she needed my help.

I heard a clatter, like stones hitting the tin roof. Ice chunks bounced and skittered across the floor. I was kicking hailstones as I ran, my ankles getting pelted. The sound became deafening. Ahead, vendors raced to squeeze into the small concession buildings. Would there be room for us?

Mimi sat cockeyed in her chair, skewed toward the row of stalls across the parking lot. "Sweet Jesus!" she cried.

I turned my head. What had been a tuft dangling from a distant cloud had become a pale twisting snake reared up on its tail. Still far away, it rose behind the last row of sheds. As it writhed, an inky dark blue rose up the chalky column.

I tried to run faster, but I slipped on a chunk of hail. If Mimi had been skinnier, I might have dragged her and the chair over on myself. Clinging to the wheelchair's grips I scraped both knees on the pavement. When I tried to get up my ankle buckled.

Someone screamed. Was it me? Was it Mimi? As the tornado swarmed toward us its roar became deafening. It was too close, we weren't going to get away. I squeezed my eyes shut. I was going to die at age twelve.

Someone wrenched me up by my arm and lifted. I was thrown over a shoulder. I smelled tobacco, sweat. My head hung down and I thump, thumped against my rescuer's back. Whoever it was kept running, pushing Mimi's wheelchair out ahead.

Hanging upside down, I saw the tornado hit the first row of market stalls. With a sound like a rifle shot, a length of the tin roof peeled up and got sucked in. Then the view was blotted out by concrete block; we were between the concession stands. I was dumped on the ground. "Danny!" I shouted, recognizing his shoes. He grabbed my arm. He was dragging me when I heard the tornado hit the second row of sheds.

The doors to both concession stands were closed. Locked, or jammed closed because they were so full. Danny shoved the wheelchair up against the door, threw an arm around me and held the doorknob with his free hand. Mimi and I clung to him, afraid the wind would tear us away.

The twister hit our wing with a roar that filled every particle of the world. I was crying, but the sound fell into the roar like a drop of water into the ocean, and the air turned solid. Sand scoured the backs of my legs. I was trying to breath through the weave of Danny's shirt when something cracked me in the calf like a hurled softball.

My calf was still stinging when my feet whipped out from under me. Like a dog jerking on a towel, the wind tried to worry me out of Danny's arms. Then, with a final shake, it opened its jaws. I slid to my knees but Danny caught me under my arms and lifted. As the retreating tornado made room for regular air, I got a whiff of the rubber scent of Danny's shirt. It smelled better than any incense Mr. Finch ever sold.

Chapter 14
One Pink Sneaker

W hoa, there, Rox." Danny gave my back a few consoling whacks. "Turn off the faucet." Then he grasped my shoulders, peeled me off his chest, and held me at arms length. "You're okay."

I wiped my nose on my sleeve. "How's Mimi?"

"She's fine," said Mimi. Her hands pressed her knees as she held herself up, which is what she does when she's having trouble breathing. The goldfish in the bag in her lap were swimming around like nothing had happened.

Danny gave the closed door a hard slap with his open hand. "Thanks for letting us in, you guys."

Then he strode to the front of the space between the concession stands.

"No!" I stumbled after him. "It could turn back!"

Danny stuck his head out. "Not hardly, take a look."

As I followed him, I heard the doors of the concession stands open. "Is it safe?" asked a voice.

The tornado had crossed the road. What was left of it wobbled and staggered. It was dropping the things it had picked up. The length of tin roofing fell with a clatter. The carcass of a dresser, minus the drawers, was hurled out by the whirlwind. The dresser spun, like a cowboy who had just taken a bullet, then fell onto its back. Little by little, the tornado became a dusty ripple in the air, and then it was gone.

Danny stepped out and took the first good look down our wing of the flea market. "We got some folks in trouble," he shouted, and he began to run. "Somebody get to the office and call 911!"

But a man who had been selling the junk out of his garage to make space for new junk whipped out a cell phone.

The others ran after Danny. I stayed with Mimi. "Are you okay, really?" That's when I noticed the grape stuck in her squirrel's-nest hairdo. I started to laugh. It sounded demented, like the laugh on a Halloween tape. I couldn't stop.

"Go ahead, mock me." I heard a whistle as she refilled her lungs. "I about died of fright. With all that stuff in the air, I couldn't breathe whatsoever." She tried to inhale again and set off a coughing jag.

"Mimi?" I put my hands on her shoulders to support her as the cough tore through her. "I wasn't laughing at you, I was laughing at your grape, see?" I plucked it out of her hair and showed her. "Are you okay?"

"Fine." She unwadded the tissue she held in her fist and wiped her teary eyes. Then she dug in the big black purse jammed between her and the arm of the chair.

"Don't smoke, Mimi! You're already filled with sand!"

Her fingers trembled as she lit up. "To calm my nerves," she said. She took a deep drag, and then waved the hand that held the cigarette in the direction of our stand. "Let's take a look at the disaster." She throttled forward. This time the chair powered right up.

We zigzagged through the field of debris left by the storm. The Gonzalez's fruit had been strewn for hundreds of feet. Exploded grapefruits and oranges littered our path. One of them had probably been the softball pitched into my calf. It was good Mimi had to go slow. I couldn't have kept up with her at top speed. It was hard to put weight on my twisted ankle. I was limping pretty bad.

As we got close to our booth we could see a drift of hailstones and shattered china piled against our capsized table. "Look at the mug," Mimi said. The ugly Oktoberfest beer stein was one of the few things still in one piece. "We can't sell it, and we can't break it." Mimi said. "Just promise you won't bury it with me, okay?"

The air was breathless and still. It smelled as if all the good in it had been used up. I looked for my stool but it was gone, so I stood, my limbs heavy and tired. I could have curled up on the concrete and closed my eyes.

Ferry Morgan's calf was bawling and bawling. In the parking lot dazed goats hobbled around, bumping into cars. Their pen, which had fallen out from under the shed, lay on its side, door popped.

"Hey," Danny shouted. "Can you roll the window down?"

I looked his way. For a second I couldn't figure out that I was looking at the underside of the Gonzalez's truck.

I'd assumed that the Gonzalezes had driven away. Instead their truck lay on its side. Using both hands, and all his muscle, Danny was unable to lift the crushed passenger door. If the door was crushed, the truck must have rolled over at least once. "Carlos?" Danny slapped the window again. "Carmen? Can you hear me?" Staring at the silent truck cab, I remembered a gizmo someone had given us to sell that could scramble an egg without cracking it open. I wanted to throw up.

But then baby Rosa began to wail. Danny pounded harder. "Please, roll the window down!"

The bright sky was reflected on the window, and then, slowly, very slowly, the patch of sky narrowed. Rosa's cry burst through the widening gap. As soon as the window was open enough, Danny plunged both arms in and lifted Rosa out. "Rox?"

The baby was all mouth, screaming so loudly her tongue vibrated. I held her against my chest but she was like a twanging spring. One second she was coiled. The next she was throwing her arms and legs out.

"Is that all the further it'll open?" Danny shouted. "Let me give it a try." He reached an arm through the partially opened window. "You're right," he said. "It's tight as a tick."

I heard Marco's voice over Rosa's crying. "I can squeeze out," he yelled.

"Not so fast, amigo. First, tell me, do you hurt anywhere?"

Marco's skinny arms shot up through the window. "I gotta get out!"

"Okay, okay." Danny dragged him up by the arms, set him on his feet, and gave him a pat on the behind.

"Ow!" Marco rubbed the spot. "I sprained my butt."

Danny hoisted him and chucked him a couple of feet in the air, then caught him in a hug. "Beats losing it, amigo."

Juan climbed out on his own. That left Mr. and Mrs. Gonzalez, both too big and heavy to squeeze out a half-open window. "Carlos? Carmen? Are you okay in there?"

A siren wailed. Danny sprinted out the other side of the shed and waved his arms. "Over here, over here." At the sound of the siren, Rosa twisted so hard I nearly dropped her.

Suddenly, I remembered Miss Louise. She had been crying for help. "Mimi," I said, putting the baby in my grandmother's lap. "Hold Rosa, okay?"

Mimi looked confused. For a second the squirming baby kind of lay there, head lower than her feet, the bag of goldfish a pillow under her back. Then Mimi seemed to notice there was a baby in her lap. "Come to Miss Marilyn," she cooed in that funny, high voice adults reserve for babies. Tucking the baby's fuzzy head under her chin, she draped Rosa across her broad bosom. Rosa let out one big *hic* and settled down.

~

Miss Louise's table lay at the edge of the concrete slab, legs up, like a dead roach. Wasps that usually buzzed the trash cans walked across slick spills of jam and tupelo honey and along the edges of the shattered glass. Blown up against a roof pole was one pink sneaker. I picked it up. I was hugging it when someone called my name.

I turned toward the voice, hugging the shoe. "Rox, you're still in one piece!" Lucy Everhart was galloping toward me. She took a slide in the jam and smashed right into me. She used the momentum to lift me off the ground in a hug. I'm nearly as tall as Lucy, and she weighs less. I was so surprised to be picked up and spun that I almost dropped the sneaker. "Am I glad to see you!" she hollered. "Let me take a look at you." She set me down for a second, then hugged me again. "I was afraid you'd gone over the rainbow."

"I'm okay." No one had ever been that glad to see me before.

"We heard about the tornado on the radio," she said. "Johnny was so worried he broke every traffic law in the book getting here."

John Martin broke every law for us? "Where is he?"

"He's helping roll that truck over. He'll be so glad to see you." Lucy looked curiously at the sneaker in my hand. "Whose shoe?"

I held the pink sneaker by one straggly lace. "Miss Louise's."

"Where is the rest of her?"

"I don't know. She was calling for help; she couldn't get out of her chair." My eyes filled with tears. "I didn't help her."

"You were busy saving Mimi, right? Come on, let's find Miss Louise and give her back her shoe."

I had to sling an arm around Lucy's neck because of my ankle. Together we hobbled out to the lot like contestants in a three-legged race.

The tornado had reparked the few cars in the front lot. None were between the lines anymore. One lay on its roof. Across the road, fence posts were snapped like toothpicks. "Miss Louise has a son named Gus," I babbled as we followed the twister's trail. "He drives her back and forth like John Martin does us. He's going to FSU on a football scholarship."

At first I was sure I was going to see Miss Louise any second, sitting in the dirt, looking surprised. "Well, that was quite a ride," she would say. "Thanks for bringing my other shoe. Now, could you give me a hand up, hon?"

We crossed the road and stepped over the twisted fence wire. In the field we kept coming across merchandise the tornado had swiped from our tables. Stuff that looked nice arranged in a flea market booth was now broken and ugly. I saw one of Mr. Finch's smoking Nubian cats. Although it was china it hadn't broken. Still holding the sneaker by its lace, I cradled the cat in the crook of my arm. *Look Mr. Finch,* I'd say. *You lost all your inventory, but here's a cat to get you started again.* Maybe it would be like a magic bean, and turn into something more.

And what would I give Gus? His mother's sneaker?

Then we found the dead starlings, wild birds that had gotten caught in the funnel. Half their feathers had been blasted off. I hugged the black china cat to my ribs so hard it hurt. The idea of finding Miss Louise barely rumpled was ludicrous. I had abandoned her, and now she was missing. "We need to tell the police about Miss Louise," I whispered.

Lucy tried to help me, but I stumbled back across the field, limping on my bad ankle. "I should've gone back," I said. "I should've."

"Did you have *time* to go back?"

"But Lucy, we're family here. We help each other."

"What if you had gone back, Rox? Then you and Mimi might be dead too."

I moaned. Lucy had said it out loud. Miss Louise was dead.

We were crossing the parking lot, me crying and crushing Mr. Finch's smoking cat into my chest, when Mrs. Yu's boat of a car pulled in. It sat low on its tires, as if all four were underinflated. The dark tinted windows reflected a sky as blue as a baby's blanket, all speckled with fleecy clouds. But that sky didn't fool me. I knew it could swallow a woman as large as a mountain and burp out nothing but a shoe.

Mrs. Yu hopped out, as quick as a small bird. She rushed around, opened the passenger door, and reached in with both hands. "You ready for upsy-daisy?"

"Ready as I'll ever be, I guess," said a voice that was usually heard singing the praises of tupelo honey.

Mr. Finch wasn't going to have a smoking Nubian cat to restart his inventory because the moment I heard that voice I dropped the cat, *smash,* along with the pink sneaker. "Miss Louise!" I hopped over to her on my good foot.

"What is it, hon?" she asked as Mrs. Yu leaned back and pulled her to her feet. "You look like you saw a ghost."

"I'm so sorry I didn't help you. I'm so *so* glad you're alive!"

"Me too. Thanks to this little lady."

Mrs. Yu clucked her tongue, saying it was nothing. "We all big family." Exactly what I had told Lucy. I had never felt closer to the people at the Show. If we could come through a tornado I guess we could come through anything.

Lucy picked up the sneaker and presented it to Miss Louise. "Thanks, hon," said Miss Louise. "I wondered where I left that. Rox, you mind helping me put it on?"

Chapter 15
Six Men in a Sailboat

Is that you, Rox?" the voice on the phone asked. "This is Marie Summers. Is your grandma handy?"

"Marie Summers," I said, passing the phone to Mimi. Who was Marie Summers? As they talked I realized it was Spice Marie from the Show. She had never had a last name before. She had never called before. It was as if the people we spent every weekend with didn't exist during the week. "Tell her we'll be there," I said, crowding Mimi. Spice Marie had to be calling about tomorrow.

Mimi covered her ear with her hand and listened. "Uh-huh," she said.

I had everything worked out for the next day. We hadn't lost too much because we were almost sold out. Our table was smashed, but we had a folding table we could bring. We could stay up late, make more wreaths. Lucy would probably help.

Mimi hung up. "They closed the Show."

I gasped. "Closed it?"

"For repairs."

"Until when?"

"It could be a while. The owners have to settle with the insurance. And Marie says if we want to get paid for our busted stuff, we can forget it. The only things covered are the buildings." She watched the three goldfish swimming laps in a mixing bowl on the kitchen table. "John Martin wants us to quit the Show anyway," she said, avoiding my eyes. "He says the tornado was a sign."

"A sign?" I knew John Martin didn't believe in signs. He only said it because he was talking to Mimi. "But we *can't* quit. We need the money."

"He'll give me more from his paycheck each week. He's worried about how you're doing in school."

"I'll do better, I promise. You still like doing the Show, don't you, Mimi?"

She winced when I grabbed her bruised arm. "Not as much as I used to."

I let go fast. "But the tornado was a freak of nature! It won't happen again. We *belong* at the Show."

"To everything there is a season." I hate it when she quotes Scripture. Who can talk back to the Bible? I hugged her instead, silently begging.

Mimi ran a weary hand down my back. "The plain truth is I'm old and I'm tired. It'll be kind of nice to have weekends off."

"But you already have weekdays off!" I couldn't believe what was happening. The Show was slipping away. It was like trying to hold water in my hands. I slid out of the hug and stepped back. "I could do the Show by myself, you know. Or maybe me and Lucy."

"Lucy wouldn't last two days. She runs on enthusiasm." I started to say something but she shushed me. "Your cousin's made up his mind. He's the man around here."

Mimi had never deferred to Grandpa Bill when he was the man around here! She had never let *anyone* dictate what would happen to her and me. "But Mimi, the Show is what we do. The two of us. We're a team."

"John Martin has his reasons." I wanted to scream, *dumb reasons,* but she weakened. "All right. Talk to him, Rox. See what you can work out. I guess I have a few trips to the Show left in me yet."

But how was I supposed to talk to him when he was off somewhere with Lucy? Mimi went to bed early. I tried to stay awake and nab him when he got home, but I fell asleep. The tornado had worn us out.

~

Our first Sunday off. We could've slept late. But bruises and all, Mimi insisted on going to church.

"Suck it in," I told her as I tugged at the back of her old blue church dress. "The sides are still a good inch apart."

"It must've shrunk," she grunted.

"Or you grew." We both had. I was having trouble breathing in the ugly yellow dress that had been squashed at the back of my closet for at least a year. "Let all your air out and hold it." I put my knee on her butt and pulled harder, trying to get the buttons and button-holes to meet.

"John Martin!" she bawled as I wrestled with her dress. "I ironed you a shirt."

"But Ma...," my cousin complained from the kitchen. "I don't have time for church. I gotta study for a test."

"Then pray you do good on the test, 'cause you're going," she shouted back. "Rox and me almost died yesterday. The least we can do is say thanks for sparing us over another day."

Heads turned as we walked up the church aisle. Charles, who was sitting with his mom, stared at my short dress and fat bare knees. I don't know what he was gawking at. It wasn't like his church clothes fit any better. His shirt cuffs hung out the ends of the sleeves of his jacket. His socks were on full display.

"Welcome back!" the church ladies chorused when we stopped in the fellowship hall for after-church coffee and cookies. Everyone said how much they'd missed Mimi's famous pecan sticky buns.

Mimi cried—and promised to bake some for next Sunday.

"You're wearing a dress," said Charles, offering me a cup of punch.

"Don't rub it in," I told him. We sat down in folding chairs by the wall. I tried to cover my knees with my froofy skirt. "I miss my overalls."

"You look nice."

"Liar." I tucked my pasty legs under the chair.

"It's kind of weird to be here, isn't it?" he said, watching Mimi and his mom sip coffee together. Since he wasn't working the Show with his dad, Charles's mom had dragged him to church too.

"I feel like we should be trying to sell these folks something," I answered. This was only the first Sunday of being off and I hated it. "Charles, we belong at the Show."

∼

Mimi was napping upstairs when I finally cornered my cousin in the living room. I could hear the thin whistle of her snore as I began giving him all the reasons he had to let me go back to work. But he cut me off.

"Forget it," he said, tying his bootlace. "You've been diddling around pulling Cs and Ds. All you think about is making things for the Show."

"And paying the bills."

He held up his hands. "Not your problem, Rox. From now on I got it covered."

He tied the second lace, then tried to go out the front door. I tackled him from behind. "Pleeeeease. Oh, please." The toes of my shoes bunched the rug up as he dragged me. *"Pleeeeease..."*

"Would ya cut it out, Rox." He pried me off. When I tried to jump back on, he clamped my arms to my sides. "Listen. I know how much the Show means to you, but you'll thank me in the long run. You and me started out at the bottom. The only way we're gonna get anywhere is to climb. So far, Rox, I don't see you climbing."

"School is easy for you." I spit the words at him. "You were *always* good at it."

"Because I work at it. Always have. And you gotta work too."

"What if I'm just dumb? All the teachers think I am." I knew I was being unfair. Miss Llewelyn claimed I had talent, which is almost the same as being smart. But I didn't want to be fair. I wanted to win.

"So what if they think you're dumb. It's your job to prove they're wrong." He lowered his voice. "You don't want to grow up to be Ma, do you?"

"How can you say anything about her? She took you in and raised you and loved you." Seen through tears, John Martin's face seemed to be dissolving.

"Aw, don't cry, Rox." He smooshed me into his chest and whacked my back, *thump, thump.* "All I'm saying is you don't want her life. You don't want to worry about every bill and not have the money to see a doctor when you need to. You know I love Ma, but loving her means taking care of her, and making her proud."

"*You* can make her proud. *I'll* help her pay the bills. Please, John Martin, please! I need to go back to the Show. I have to go back…"

He grabbed me by the shoulders. "Not until the grades go up." He gave me a little shake. "It's for your own good, Rox."

I blinked back the tears and remembered: I was the one who could sell a saddle to a horse. "If I bring my grades up, can I go back to the Show?"

He cocked his head, like it was some kind of trick. "Bring 'em up how much?"

Start low, I told myself. Find the bottom. "All Bs and Cs."

"All Bs or better," he countered.

"You're kidding, right? Okay, okay. Bs or better, and *then* you'll let me go back?"

"One day a week."

"What about for all As?"

"Still one day."

"That's your best offer, one day a week?"

He let go of my shoulders and crossed his arms. "Yup. That's my best offer."

"Bs or better…" Suddenly I remembered math and I knew the deal was a disaster. "Can I have one C, please?" I begged, desperate to renegotiate.

"Nope."

My midterm progress report had been crappy. "It won't be this semester, it can't."

"Show me it's going the right way. Bring me the grades, and we'll talk about it. And one more thing, Rox. You go to school every day. No stomachaches, no scratchy throats, no staying home to keep Ma company. Do we have a deal?"

For a second I just stared at the hand he held out. It was a lousy deal—but it was the best I would get from John Martin. "Deal," I said, and we shook on it.

~

I grabbed ahold of the banister and hopped up the stairs on my good foot, pounding the steps in protest. It was so unfair. I would have to work like crazy to get back half of what I had had all along, but I had no choice. Half was better than none. The first draft of Edison was due on Monday, minimum five pages. Five isn't much if you write big. I had planned to do my five pages at the Show. But to get a B or better I had to do more like ten pages. Maybe even twelve. I slammed the bedroom door behind me.

I wrote nine pages in a couple of hours. But Edison wasn't the real problem; the real problem was math. The real problem was always math. Except for making change at the Show, math was a language I didn't understand.

Usually I worked on my bed lying on my stomach, but I thought sitting at a desk might help. I cleared off the china figurines and dusted the top with my sleeve.

A math book, a pencil, a lamp. The desk looked deserted. I chose one of my favorite dogs, a Scottie, and put it on the corner of my desk. The china dog looked perky and eager. He was just waiting for me to zip through my math. Then I opened the book to page eighty-seven.

"Word problems," I groaned. Tears stung my eyes. It was the worst case possible. I could never figure out word problems. A man got on a train, or an egg fell off the Empire State Building, or two runners started at opposite ends of town, and the question was how fast, how far, what time? Where did the answers come from? It didn't seem to help to imagine the egg spinning end over end until it splatted on the pavement. It didn't help to wonder where the man on the train was going.

I looked at the china Scottie for encouragement, then read the first problem. I had no idea how to solve it, and I never would. I put my head down on the desk. I would stay like that until I was old enough to quit school. Fourteen, if Charles was right. In math, a B or better was impossible. But without that B, I would never get to go back to the one place where I knew exactly what to do.

~

"John Martin?" I stood in front of him, hugging my math book. "Let's say there's this man on a train going from Pittsburgh to Salt Lake City and he leaves Pittsburgh at nine in the morning."

He didn't look up from his work. "Read the examples at the front of the chapter."

"A man on a train is going from Pittsburgh to Salt Lake City," I repeated.

He looked at me over his reading glasses, impatient. Then he must have seen the tears that were ready to spill. "Pittsburgh to Salt Lake?" He leaned back in his chair and tipped it up on its back legs. "That means he'd cross two time zones."

"Time zones!" I collapsed into the seat next to his. "Don't make this any harder than it already is." I opened the book to page eighty-seven and set it in front of him.

"Which one don't you get?"

I pointed. "Problem number one."

In five minutes he realized that I didn't have a clue about how to solve word problems, but he didn't yell. Instead he kept asking, "What's the real question?"

"Something about going from Pittsburgh to Salt Lake City on a train."

"But what?"

"I don't know. How fast?"

"Now you're cooking! And how would you express how fast?"

What kind of crazy question was that? "In English?"

He knocked on my head with his knuckles. "Wake up, Rox. How do you measure how fast?"

I wiped my nose on the back of my hand. "Miles per hour?" I whispered.

"Bingo! Miles per hour!"

It turned out that it didn't matter if it was a man on a train or a dog on a train—there didn't even have to be a train. In each case it was a question of distance, speed, and time. Sometimes you multiplied, sometimes you divided. "It's like writing a sentence with numbers," he explained. "Now do the last three yourself." And he went back to his own homework.

I slid the book over so it was right in front of me. I took a deep breath. *Six men in a sailboat were headed east traveling five knots...* I read it through and asked myself what John Martin had asked each time: what is the question here—other than what the heck is a knot? With a shaky hand, I began to write a number sentence about six men in a boat headed east. I left out the six men, the boat, and the direction. I kept the five knots, which I figured had to be the speed. That was all that mattered.

The pencil was slipping in my sweaty fingers when I finished the last problem. I set it down on the open book and folded my hands. I wanted my cousin to check, and I was afraid to have him check. Something was wrong. Word problems had begun to make sense.

I didn't say a thing, and he kept scribbling away, writing number sentences and number paragraphs of his own. Finally, he glanced up. "Ya stuck, Rox?"

I turned my book toward him and slid the paper over.

His eyes skimmed problem eleven, *six men in a sailboat...* He glanced at my answer, then looked over at me. He read problems twelve and thirteen. He read my number sentences and pushed the book away. "Rox." He reached out like he was going to knock on my head for being a doof again, but he only rapped once. "I think you got it," he said. "You understand."

I folded the paper into my book and stood, knees shaking. I had done one page of baby math, while other kids in my grade got ready to take big bites out of algebra. But still, I had done it right.

Me, the mathematically challenged Roxanne Piermont.

~

I couldn't sleep. One page of elementary math, even done right, began to seem like nothing. The longer I lay there not sleeping, the more nothing it became. It was like sucking one of Mr. Tully's hard candies until even the taste was gone.

I was going to have to work like crazy every day to pull my grades up. Except for the fact it would get me back to the Show, it wasn't worth it. I had serious doubts about John Martin's get-ahead plan. He was wrong if he thought bad spelling or poor math skills could keep a person glued where they were. My mother, Helen, was lousy in the school department. It hadn't kept her from flying away.

Mimi coughed in the next room. I waited for her to call, "Rox? Can you get me a glass of water, two cubes?" But the coughing stopped. When it had been quiet for a while, I tiptoed to my dresser and felt around under the underwear. Reading about Helen would get me away from my own problems, and maybe Annarose was right; maybe she'd improve as the diary went on.

If she didn't, I could always stuff her back in the drawer.

May 26
Dear Diary,

    Guess what? I got a sumer job babysiting Dr Leonards kids. He's a professer at FSU. The Leonards pay in-town prices— $1.50 an hour for 40 hours a week!!! I'll put all of it away for a tiket somewhere. Maybe Hollywood. With makeup I can pass for 16 at least.

        —almost out of here Helen

June 10
Dear Diary,

    The Leonard kids are so cute! Ethan is 4 and Emily is 5. I'm teaching them to swim. (They have a pool, not the plastic kind ether). Dr Leonard wears a white shirt and necktie every day. They drink wine when they get home and ask me about my day. So elegant!!!

    There house has absolutly everything. Sometimes I just open the cubbards and stare at the rows of Pepprige Farm cookies. Milanos are my favorites!!!

    They have all different kinds of cheese too—not just mushy old Velveeta. The kids have so many toys it makes me feel bad for Spud. I wish I could take a truck home for him. They wouldn't miss it.

    Guess what? Today Mrs. Leonard taut me how to make bread. Ma says why bother when you can buy it off the shelf. But Mrs. Leonard doesn't like to feed the kids perzervatives. Baking bread is fun.

        —Helen

So *that* was how Helen learned to bake bread. I knew she hadn't learned from Mimi. Mimi says making bread is a mess because the dough gets all up under her rings; she prefers Sunbeam.

I bet the Everharts had all kinds of cheeses and shelves loaded with fancy cookies too. If they'd offered any of that stuff to John Martin he probably said, "No thank you," not sure how to use the little knife on the cheese dish, afraid of sprinkling crumbs on the rug.

June 30
Dear Diary,

Ma about scared me to death. When Mrs Leonard dropped me off Ma was blubbering and couldn't hardly talk. Seems like Spud was poking around in our yard with a stick and he put it rite in a bees nest!!! He got stung about a hundred times and swole all up and quit breathing. Pop rushed him to the hospital but he almost dyed!!!! I gave Ma my babysiting money to help pay the bill. $187!!! She didn't even have to ask. I don't feel bad about it. Theres lots more money in the world than Ma and Pop think.

—Helen

I closed the cover of my mother's diary and slid it back in the drawer. It was the perfect place to stop. Helen had helped Mimi when she needed money. It was kind of like what I did for her by working the Show. Maybe Helen had some good in her after all.

Chapter 16
What Popularity
Feels Like

At school I am invisible. Not as invisible as Annarose or Grady—the bigger you are the less anyone sees you. Still, no one had ever noticed when I got dropped off until the Monday after the tornado. At first I thought it was a coincidence that Joelle, Sara, George Daniel, and all the other popular creeps were hanging around the place where I always get out.

"Looks like your pals are waiting for you," my cousin said.

"Go a little farther." I barely moved my lips.

George Daniel trotted up as I climbed out of the truck a few feet past them. "Hey, I heard about the tornado at the flea market. Joelle says you work there sometimes. You weren't there, were you?"

I fell back a step on the foot with the twisted ankle. "Yeah, I was there."

"Told ya." Joelle twisted a strand of hair around her fingers. "So, what was it like, Rox?"

She was concentrating on me too hard. She was sure to notice one side of my overalls was gappy because I was missing a button and that the ace bandage on my ankle was old and scuzzy. "Charles was there too, weren't you, Charles?" I said, hoping to spread the attention out. Charles was on the bench reading a comic, his long bangs falling over his face. When he looked up I was limping his way, leading a crowd of popular kids. He dropped the comic.

"Here you go, Charlie." While George made a big show out of picking it up, I sat down quick and hid the place where the button was missing with my notebook. I crossed my ankles so the Ace bandage didn't show too much.

"So, would one of you please tell me what it was like?" Joelle coaxed. "Come on, Charles!" She rested a hand on his shoulder.

Charles was barely breathing. It was as if a beautiful butterfly had landed on him. "I wasn't actually there when it hit," he admitted. "My dad and I cleared out."

"But Charles was the one who ran around warning the rest of us," I said.

"*Ran* around...?" George raised his eyebrows.

Joelle's butterfly hand flitted away. It went back to playing with her hair. As she turned her green eyes on me, Charles stared at the spot where her hand had been.

"But *you* were there, Rox. Tell us about it." She looked deep into me, so kind, so interested. Maybe I had been wrong about her all along.

"The tornado was huge," I blurted out. "At first it was pale, like smoke, but then it must've touched down because it turned dark." To keep her liking me, I rushed to spill everything that had happened. "It was the loudest thing I ever heard."

Sara Michaels hugged herself. "Was it coming straight at you?"

I nodded, "Uh-huh. Straight. And the only place we had to go was the concession stands."

"They're concrete," Charles added, but no one looked at him.

"I was pushing my grandma's wheelchair, only just as the tornado crossed the parking lot next to the flea market, I fell."

By now Joelle was hanging onto Sara's arm. "You fell?"

"Yes. With the tornado coming straight for me. I thought I was dead. But at the last second someone picked me up."

Joelle and Sara traded meaningful looks. "Someone picked you up?"

"It was Danny Swain."

"The Tire King," Charles added helpfully.

Sara stifled a laugh.

"But that wasn't the worst thing that happened!" I was struggling to hold onto my new-found status. "When we reached the concessions the doors were closed. Locked! The tornado swept me off my feet and almost blew me away. Danny held onto me."

"You mean the Tire King?" Sara asked, covering her mouth to suppress a giggle.

"That's right."

"And he kept you from *blowing away?*" Sara and Joelle shared a look that said, we're best friends and we have skinny, cute-girl secrets you'll never know. Their secrets were as secret as something written on a billboard. There was a chance they were giggling about Danny, the Tire King, but it was unlikely. When you're big you realize that everything is about your size.

Bored with me and my stupid version of the tornado, Sara suddenly squealed, "Look, there's Kristy. I heard the roof got blown off her uncle's garage." She swung Joelle away from the bench and the two of them trotted after Kristy. George and all the others followed them, leaving Charles and me like trash dropped on the ground.

"Oh, by the way, Rox." Joelle turned and walked backward. "You lost a button."

My eyes stung hot. "Who cares what they think," I told Charles. "Joelle and her crowd would pull the wings off butterflies!"

"So, that's what it feels like," Charles said, gazing after them.

"That's what *what* feels like?"

"Popularity."

I wanted to shake him. "That wasn't popularity. They were only interested in the tornado."

"Better than nothing," said Charles glancing at his shoulder.

"She likes George, not you."

He flipped the pages of his comic, holding it in front of his face. "I know that," he mumbled.

"Then don't act like such a dork in front of her. Don't drool." I pulled this week's spelling list out of my pack. "Can you quiz me on spelling?"

"Why?" His voice came from behind the comic. "You do okay at spelling."

"I have to pull my grades up if I ever want to go back to the flea market."

He lowered the comic. "Your grandma won't let you go back to the flea market?"

"John Martin won't."

"Bummer." He took the list out of my hand. "Word number one, 'demonstrate'."

I got through the first three words fine, but everything about school seemed harder now, even things I was okay at, like spelling. Usually, I didn't even study for the test. There were always a couple of trick words on the list, ones that weren't spelled the way they sounded, but I could get them both wrong and still get an eighty.

Charles read word four. "Locomotion."

"*L-O-C-A-M-O-T-I-O-N.*" It didn't feel quite right, but I was hoping.

Charles shook his head. "Our first contestant has one more chance to spell the word 'locomotion' correctly." Then he whispered, "No *A*."

"But you say it with an *A*. The list is wrong."

"Yeah," he said. "Life stinks. Try again."

I spelled it with an *O* this time. I couldn't afford to spell *better* than the list. I needed a 100 percent every time so I could bring it home to my cousin. Spelling was one place I could get hundreds. You don't have to be smart to spell.

"And now," Charles announced, "playing for the Amana washer-dryer, contestant number one, Roxanne Piermont, will spell 'dehydration'."

"I know this," I said. "I do." But it was gone. I tried to remind myself by reading the word upside down.

Charles flipped the list over. "Is contestant number one trying to cheat? Just spell it, ma'am."

"D-E...H-I..."

"Ehhhhh!" Charles buzzed me out.

I buried my head in my arms.

Charles rattled on. "As a special thank-you for being our guest, contestant number one gets a year's supply of kitty litter."

"What's wrong with Rox?" I hadn't heard the bus pull up, but that was Annarose's high little voice. "Charles, what did you do to Rox?"

"Hey, don't look at me," he said. "I offered her a year's supply of free kitty litter."

$\sim$

At ten o'clock, contestant number one took the test. She nailed loco-motion and dehydration—and then blew testimony. She spelled it testamony. The *A* from locomotion had to go somewhere.

"I usually get an eighty," I said, showing my ninety to John Martin at supper. "I studied hard."

He nodded once.

"I just want to point out to you," I said, as I stuck my spelling test up on the refrigerator, "that this is a B or better."

"How about math?" he asked. "You have math homework tonight?"

The math book lurked at the bottom of my pack, waiting to get me. "I could probably use some help."

Chapter 17
Local History

On Thursdays I had always encouraged any little pain or sniffle that might give me an excuse to dodge school and the Smile Mile. But after John Martin's order to pull up my grades, my stomach ached all the time. My heart raced. One minute it seemed as if I was getting a cold, the next I itched all over. I woke up the first Thursday of the new B-or-better Rox, symptoms raging. I felt so bad I wondered if I was sick for real.

Mimi took my face in her hands at the breakfast table. "You look pretty puny, Rox. Stay home with me."

"We're starting a new unit in science," I said.

John Martin looked up from his plate of scrambled eggs. "Does that mean you're going to go?"

"I guess."

Mimi looked disappointed. I could tell she wanted company. If I stayed home we'd watch game shows and soap operas, play cards and toast Pop Tarts. But the good old days of keeping Mimi company on Thursdays were over.

I dragged myself out to the truck. As soon as we started, I turned on the radio and spun the dial.

"What are you looking for?" asked John Martin.

"Weather."

He peered through the windshield. "Not a cloud in the sky," he reported. "Looks like it'll be sunny all day." He started to whistle.

Sunny was fine with him. He was pouring concrete. But I was running the Smile Mile. If I had been smart I would've kept the Ace bandage on, but it looked so cruddy I took it off on Tuesday. Since I'd used up going to the nurse, rain was my only possible salvation.

I had completely forgotten it was Halloween until I saw my first teacher in the hall. By the time you reach seventh, Halloween isn't much. Only the teachers really dress up. Miss Llewelyn came bustling down the hall carrying a stuffed sheep. When George Daniel asked who she was supposed to be, she shook the sheep at him. "Little Bo Peep, who else?"

Most Thursdays I concentrated my will on changing the weather, but today I couldn't. I had to pay attention in class—which was hard because Mr. Farrell was wearing Groucho Marx glasses complete with plastic nose, bushy eyebrows, and mustache. Yet somehow, even without my mental energy, clouds formed over the Gulf of Mexico, and a wind brought them in. At first they were separate. Then, like dumplings on a pot of stew, they began to swell together. A peal of thunder rattled the classroom windows.

"You think it could actually rain?" Annarose whispered.

"Have we ever been that lucky?" I whispered back.

Tiny drops freckled the windows. "I feel it, Rox. Our luck is changing!"

~

Lucy pointed to the torn knee of my overalls. "What happened to you?"

"I fell running the Smile Mile this morning. Coach made us run in the rain."

"What rain?" said my cousin. "It was barely spittin'."

"It was *raining* and the track was slick." I picked up his paper plate. If there had been anything on it, I would have accidentally spilled it in his lap, but all that was left was a big old grease spot from the chicken-fried steak.

He immediately filled the empty space on the table with a calculus book and pretended to study, but when Lucy reached over him to take his fork, he kissed her arm, right in the fold of the elbow.

"Just what Lucy wants," I said. "Grease on her arm." She kissed him behind an ear. "Jeez, you guys…"

They wouldn't do that stuff with Mimi in the room, but Mimi had excused herself after a couple of bites of dinner and shuffled off to the living room to watch TV.

Lucy washed the glasses and silverware. Between blasts of water, fake laughter bubbled in from the living room. Sometimes Mimi laughed along; sometimes she coughed along. Each time Mimi hacked, Lucy's shoulders pinched. "Cigarettes," she mumbled, scrubbing at a fork. Mimi coughed again. "You need a drink?" Lucy yelled.

"I wouldn't mind one."

I brought her the usual, water with two cubes. When I got back in the kitchen Lucy and John Martin jumped apart. Lucy giggled and pointed to a spoon in the drainer. "Last one!"

I dried the last spoon. "I need another Edison source for my bibliography," I announced.

"You look at everything in the school library?" John Martin asked.

"Everything's checked out." I threw the last spoon in the drawer. "I need to go to the *public* library." How badly did he want me to pull up my grades? Bad enough to quit studying and smooching and drive me?

My cousin raised his book. "Tomorrow night, Rox. After my test."

"The library won't be open tomorrow night."

"Okay, Johnny-boy, toss me the keys," Lucy said.

He reached out and hooked her by the pocket, then roped his arms around her waist. "Come on, Luce, we have work to do."

"You call that work?" I asked. They were dangerously close to kissing again.

"Rox needs to go to the library," Lucy said, unlatching his arms. "I'll take my calculus book along."

134

As soon as we climbed in the truck, Lucy chucked her book over the back of the seat. "Where to?" she asked, jackrabbitting the truck into forward.

"We have to drive through Crawfordville almost all the way to Medart," I said.

"No problem." She winked. "It'll give me a chance to drive the pickup." We rattled over the washboard ruts of Johnson Carter road, emptying the puddles in big sprays. "Yahoo!" she yelled.

"What are your folks like?" I asked. For a girl who lived in town, she seemed to get a kick out of the most rednecky things.

"Old," she said, jouncing onto the paved road and stomping the pedal. "They were almost forty when I was born." That'd make them about Mimi's age. *Really* old. "My dad's a doctor, and my mother teaches violin at FSU. I love them, but they are *so* dignified."

I snagged two Starlight Mints as they slid across the dashboard. I unwrapped one for her and one for me. "How about brothers and sisters?" I asked, passing her a mint.

"I don't have any." She popped the candy in her mouth. "I'm an only."

"That's how come you have all those pretty clothes. You don't have to share."

"I wouldn't mind some brothers and sisters, even if I did have to share. I'd love to have someone to make a little noise with." Even though she was speeding, she took her eyes off the road and turned to me. "Hey, I have an idea! You want to be honorary sisters?"

"Yeah, okay."

"All right!" she said. "Spit on your hand and shake."

"Aren't we supposed to cut ourselves and mix blood?"

"I pass out at the sight of blood." So we spat, shook hands, and rubbed the spit off on the fuzzy dice hanging from the rearview mirror. Our first sister-secret was a vow not to tell John Martin we'd slimed his dice.

"Yahoo!" She pushed the pedal to the floor and we flew, the engine complaining loudly.

I shouted to her. "I bet when this old truck rattles up, your folks think you're dating Jethro from *The Beverly Hillbillies!*"

"They think Johnny's grammar's a little rough," she admitted.

"John Martin talks okay."

She quick-punched my shoulder, a move she'd learned watching my cousin and me. "That's what I told them. I said, 'He talks good.' My mother said, 'Well, he certainly is a good-looking young man.' And I said, 'Yeah, Mother, he's a hunk.'"

"A hunk?" I punched my honorary sister back. "John Martin is dog meat!"

"Nuh-uh!" she shouted.

"Yes, huh!"

Lucy acted all mad, but I knew she wasn't. She just wanted to make a little noise.

~

Lucy parked in front of the library and we fell out. "Clear up to the door lock," she said, admiring the fan of mud on the truck's side panel.

"It's the Mona Lisa of muddy doors," I agreed. "Hey, you forgot your calculus book." She dug it out from behind the seat, but when we got inside she didn't open it. Instead, she roamed the library while I hunted Edison sources.

Creepy organ music came from the community room. It got louder when the door opened and a witch stuck her head out. "Myrtle?" the witch called to one of the women at the desk. "I forgot the juice boxes. Be a hon and get them for me? We're right in the middle of a game of Musical Coffins."

Turned out, the public library was out of Edison too, but they had a couple of encyclopedias our school didn't, and computers, so I could go out on the web. An e-source would look great on my bibliography.

I was checking out a site on inventions that changed the world when Lucy rushed over. "Big news!" She spun a chair, straddled it, and sat down hard. After a glare from the man at the next computer, she lowered her voice. "That little room at the back belongs to the Historical Society."

"They have Edison stuff?"

"Forget Edison. Your mother went to Wakulla High, didn't she?"

"Yes. But what does—"

"Yearbooks!" she whispered. "There might be a picture."

"What if she didn't graduate?" I whispered back.

"What if she did?"

My heart went *ka-wump*. "Would they let us look?"

"Can't hurt to ask."

The woman in the Historical Society office was putting her eyeglasses back in their case. "I'm about to lock up," she said. "This isn't part of the public collection, you know."

"Please." Lucy smiled. "She's doing important research on Wakulla County history, it'll only take a minute. I appeal to you as a historian."

The woman hesitated. I could tell she liked being called a historian. "What does she need?"

"The 1990 Wakulla High yearbook," Lucy said.

"History, huh?" she grumbled. "You wouldn't have any family members who graduated in '90, would you?"

"No ma'am, not that I know of," I said as she checked my hands to be sure they were clean.

"Be quick, okay?" she said, giving me the yearbook. "My TV show comes on in fifteen minutes."

Lucy and I parked on the sofa right outside the door of the Historical Society office. "You find her," I said, thrusting the book at Lucy.

"Parsons, Parton, Pearson." Lucy flipped a page. "Whoa!" She fell back against the flabby sofa cushions.

"What? What?"

"Take a look at Helen May Piermont, Sis."

All I could do was stare.

"Takes your breath away, doesn't she?" Lucy whispered.

Helen's long, wavy hair hung loose around her shoulders—it looked like it had made it *way* past the middle of her back. She was smiling, not a big cheesy grin or anything, but smiling enough so that you could see her straight, white teeth. Her eyes were dewy. Dewy eyes are what romance novel heroines have. And so did my mother.

She wore a white blouse—all the girls did—but one of Helen's buttons didn't match the others. It had four holes instead of two. It wasn't a big difference. She'd lost a button and Mimi had sewn on the closest match she could find in the button box. Still, I hoped the other girls hadn't noticed. Girls with nice clothes think they're the fashion police. But did it matter what they said if you were as pretty as Helen? It was hard to believe there was a prettier girl at Wakulla High.

I flipped to Laura Brandt's picture and saw a pretty girl who looked something like Joelle, only skinnier. Mrs. Tully was insane! Joelle was deluded! Even with all her eyebrows plucked out, Helen May Piermont would make Laura Brandt look like barf. I flipped back and stared at my mother again.

This time I read the words under her picture: Helen May Piermont, "Ellie." Class flirt. Long hair and fast cars...bothered by small town life...Favorite expression: "Oh, those boys!" Under most of the other students' pictures were lists of activities like Glee Club and Debating Society, but Helen didn't have any. I remembered what Mrs. Tully had said. Ellie was restless.

Lucy cleared her throat. The Historical Society lady was putting on her sweater. "Just one more thing," I said. I wanted to see what Mrs. Tully looked like when she was still Helen's friend, Lynda Smathers. Was she really a stuffed candy box?

I flipped to the *S* names. Yup, she was. To make matters worse, her nickname was "Chipmunk."

But her picture was easier to look at than my mother's. She seemed more like a regular person. Under her photo it said, "Plans to teach…loves small children…dancing barefoot at Wakulla Springs." Favorite expression: "Don't make me crazy!" She had plenty of activities: Future Homemakers, Teacher's Aide, Pep Club, Decorating Committee, Big Sisters.

What had happened to her? She wasn't a teacher. She had a job arranging flowers for brides and dead people. And she didn't look like she'd danced barefoot anywhere in a long, long time.

But when I closed the book, it was Lynda Smather's face I saw clearly in my mind, not my mother's. Helen's face was so perfect it hurt, like staring at the sun. Lynda Smathers looked like someone I might know, or even grow up to be.

"Find what you were looking for?" asked the historian, holding out a hand.

"Thank you," said Lucy. "She did."

~

On the way home, Lucy kept calling me "Sis," which I liked, until she asked me if I was reading the diary yet. I lied and said no. As her honorary sister I should have been able to share everything, but I couldn't, at least not yet. I left her at the kitchen table, cramming calculus with John Martin. I gave Mimi a quick kiss and went up to my room.

I tried to concentrate on math but the picture of my mother shimmered in my mind. Finally, I retrieved her diary.

There was only one more entry in Helen's diary for the summer at the Leonards': her fourteenth birthday.

August 22
Dear Diary,
14 feels different from 13. Much older. I'm about to start high school!!! Ma made me a cake. I ate a piece to be polite but Mrs. Leonard had already brung a bakery cake from town with my name and pink icing roses on top.

Since next week is back to school the Leonards gave me a birthday thanks for working present. A neckless with a little gold Eyefull tower on it from Paris France!!! Mrs. Leonard made me promise to work extra hard in school this year so I could go to France someday and see the tower for myself.

I crossed my fingers and said yes. I'd rather marry some rich guy.

—Helen

Milton met me at the door when I got off the bus the next day. I scratched his belly. "I'm home, Mimi! Guess what? I turned in Edison. Twelve pages plus the bibliography. That calls for ice cream with Reddi Wip and jimmies, bananas and fudge sauce, right?" The house was silent. "Mimi?" I stuck my head in the living room. The TV was on but the sound was off. Maybe she was napping. I listened for her scratchy cough as I ran up the stairs.

"Mimi?" Milton butted the backs of my thighs when I stopped in her door. The afghan on her bed was rumpled. "See? She took a nap." I went to the next logical place, but the bathroom door was open, the room empty. I picked up the can of hairspray that stood on the edge of the sink. Hairspray meant she'd gone out. "Where'd she go, Milt? And how'd she get there?" The only car we owned was John Martin's pickup, and Mimi didn't even drive.

Milton barked once and galloped down the stairs. "Show me, Milt!" I took the stairs two at a time. "Mimi!" I shouted, stepping out the back door. Milton gave one loud, *Whuff!* The only answer was the rustle of dry grape leaves.

I went back in and checked for her purse. The big black suitcase that usually hung on the knob of the pantry door was gone.

"It's not like she'd wander off." I tried to imagine Mimi walking down the dirt road, purse slung over her arm, hair done up real nice. Spice Marie told us that sometimes in the middle of the night, her mother dresses up like she's going to church and starts walking. But then, Spice Marie's mother can't remember how to use a light switch anymore. Mimi's body may be falling apart, but her brain works fine.

"Did someone pick her up?" I asked Milt. He rolled over on his back for another belly scratch. All of Mimi's closest friends had dumped her when she quit going to church. They'd probably come around again now that we were attending, but not this fast. Jesus might take Mimi back, no questions asked. But the church ladies were less forgiving.

I had to get hold of John Martin. Sooner or later he'd have to pick up Lucy. I could catch him there, or at least leave a message. I pulled the Tallahassee phone book down off the refrigerator.

There were five Everharts listed, but I knew which one it was. Dr. and Mrs. Wilton Everhart. "Fancy name," I told Milt. "Dr. Wilton Everhart. Bet he holds his pinkie up when he drinks his coffee." I was talking to a dog about pinkies because I didn't want to make the call.

I dialed the first three numbers, *beep, beep, beep,* then I heard the purr of tires moving slowly up the driveway. I slammed the phone down and ran to the window.

A gleaming silver car with tinted windows was gliding toward our house. I pulled the curtain back, just a little, as the car stopped. "Hush now, Milton. Don't you dare bark."

The passenger door was flung open. "Two times a day! Three times a day!" said a familiar crabby voice. "With food! Without food! How the heck am I supposed to keep track?" And Mimi heaved herself out of the seat.

The driver's side door opened with a polite little *click.* "I'll make you a chart, Mrs. Piermont. It'll be easy," said Lucy, climbing out.

Milton and I rushed the door. "Where have you been?"

Mimi walked slowly, the handles of the stuffed plastic bags cutting into her arm fat, her ninety-pound purse whomping her thigh with each step. "Ask Miss Busybody here," she huffed.

"We've been to the doctor," Lucy said.

"Who just happens to be her daddy." Mimi put a hand on the

banister of the porch steps, too winded to climb. "Imagine how I felt, sitting there in the altogether wrapped in a paper dress that didn't even close in back, saying 'How do you do, pleased to meet you.'"

Lucy and Milton formed a train behind Mimi. Lucy pushed Mimi up the steps; Milton followed, licking Lucy's ankles. "My father sees people in the altogether everyday," said Lucy, ignoring the dog.

"Not me, he don't." Mimi lurched through the door and swooned into a kitchen chair. Her bags hit the floor.

"Okay, Milton, okay. I love you too." Lucy's ankles were glistening with dog spit. When she dropped to her heels and hugged him, the dog was so happy he wriggled all over. "You're like hugging an earthquake, you know that, Milt?"

"What's in the bags?" I asked.

Mimi shook her head sadly. "Every drug known to modern medicine except the ones that get you happy."

I took a peek. "How come there are so many little bottles?"

"I don't know. The nurse said, 'Here,' so I took 'em."

I pulled out a larger flat box. "The patch," I read. "For smoking cessation." I stared at my grandmother. "Are you going to quit smoking, Mimi?"

"Yes, she is," said Lucy.

"Maybe, maybe not. Last I checked it was still my body," Mimi complained.

Mimi quit smoking? I couldn't imagine it. When things got busy at the Show, she stuck an extra behind her ear, to have it handy. Half the time when she talked, a cigarette wagged on her lip.

"Now, if you'll excuse me." Mimi shoved herself to her feet. "After all that poking and pinching, I've got to rest my dignity." She climbed the stairs slowly, announcing, "Wish I had me one of them riding chairs to get up these steps."

As soon as I heard her door close I was all over Lucy. "What did your daddy say? Is she all right?"

Lucy straddled the chair Mimi had just vacated. "He says she has emphysema. Don't look so shocked, Sis. Everyone who smokes for any length of time gets it. She has arthritis, plus half a dozen other things, but her heart's good and strong. If she does what my father told her, she'll feel a whole lot better."

"But she doesn't have anything life threatening?"

"Emphysema *is* life threatening. That's why she just has to quit smoking."

"I don't know.... Smoking is what she does. It's like a job."

"People quit smoking every day. She'll do fine." She didn't know Mimi and her cigarettes. Mimi had pneumonia once. Cigarettes were off-limits, but she would wheedle me to sneak her one. "Our little secret," she'd say, making me her accomplice. I wanted my grandmother alive, with plenty of oxygen swimming around in her blood, but this was going to be hard.

Mimi's purse lay on its side. I picked up the pack of cigarettes that stuck out the top. "Four left."

Lucy reached for the pack. "I'll get rid of them."

"Let her smoke them," I said, hiding them behind my back. "It'll give her a chance to say good-bye."

"Say good-bye...to cigarettes?"

"I know it sounds funny, but whenever Mimi's bored or lonely, a cigarette keeps her company. During the day, when we're away, she fills up the ashtrays. Let her have these last four."

"Okay. Just those four. We have to be tough, Rox. " Lucy bustled over to the fridge and stuck her head in. "Her diet has to change too. Less fat, more vegetables. It'll be good for the whole family."

I heard Mimi's voice in my head: How does *she* know what's good for our family? "Is that your parent's car?" I asked, looking out the window.

"Mine. My father picked it. *Consumer Reports* said a Beamer was safe and reliable. I wanted a Harley."

"How come you never drive it here?" It would save John Martin gas if she did.

"A BMW's not much of a mud car." Reflected clouds drifted

across the black glass windshield. Take away the patchy brown grass and the gnomes and it could have been a commercial. Lucy's car didn't belong in our yard.

"Nothing but a few bendy carrots," Lucy reported. All I could see was the back of her designer jeans. Like the BMW, the jeans clashed with their surroundings, which happened to be a fridge my cousin had re-enameled with a can of white appliance paint.

We were at the table trying to make a medicine chart for Mimi when John Martin came home. Lucy rushed over to him, went up on her toes, and planted a kiss smack on his lips. "Sorry you drove all that way. I saw a chance to get Mimi in to see my dad, and I took it."

"Your mom told me." He wrapped his arms around her waist. "All I want to know is, how'd you get her to go? I been trying to talk her into seeing Doc Winslow for months."

Lucy made a face. "The pediatrician?"

John Martin looked offended. "He's our doctor."

"Come on, Johnny." She gave him a push. "A pediatrician?"

"He goes to our church," I blurted out. "He gives us a fellowship discount."

John Martin shot me a look that said anything about money is family business, then he turned back to Lucy. "So, how *did* you get her to go?"

"Easy," Lucy answered. "She wanted to go."

"Well, knock me over!" He lifted his ball cap and ran a hand over his buzzed hair. "You're kidding me."

"You know all those weird symptoms she's been having? You're not the only one who was scared about them." Then she gave him the news about the emphysema. I held up the patches.

John Martin whistled between his teeth. "Getting her to quit's not going to be easy."

"Too bad," Lucy said. "She's got to do it."

"We'll do what we can," he said, and then he grinned. "Ma can put up one heck of a fight when there's a cigarette at stake."

"This isn't funny, Johnny. She has to quit." He laced his fingers

145

through hers and kissed her nose, but she pulled back. "You need to take this seriously."

"I do, I do. But keep in mind what we're up against. Now, how much do I owe your dad?"

"Nothing."

"What do you mean, nothing?" He drove his thumbs deep into his pockets and rolled his shoulders forward. "Doctor's visits cost. Then there's the medicine."

"The medicine is all free samples. And my father does pro bono work all the time," she said. "It's worth it if the patients follow his orders and get well."

"What's pro bono?" I asked.

"It's when someone works for nothing," said John Martin. "Charity." He stood up tall. "Ma's not a charity case, and she's not real good at following orders. How much do I owe?"

Lucy stood up tall too, although it wasn't as impressive. "Nada, zip, zero. Quit being stubborn."

"May as well tell him to quit breathing," I said, but she was being stubborn too, trying to force John Martin to accept handouts. John Martin liked to do for himself, even when he couldn't afford to.

He turned and stared out the window at the silver Beamer. "All right, Lucy Everhart," he said at last. "Just this once. But for the record, taking charity is not what I do. It don't sit right."

"Johnny, Johnny." She turned him away from the gleaming car and touched her nose to his. "We have more important things to worry about than your big old pride. Sit down at this table. Rox and I are in the middle of a Mimi Summit."

"What's this?" John Martin tried to read Lucy's medicine chart but couldn't. Arrows went this way and that. There were cross-outs galore. "Let's divide it up by times of day," he suggested, flipping her chart and starting over on the back.

I tried to help Lucy make a healthy food list. But, according to Lucy, none of the things I suggested were healthy. Most of the items on the Lucy-approved list were green. "Give me a little time," John

Martin said, leaning over to read the list. "I'll grow what you need in the garden. Except for canned peas and collards, Ma don't cook anything green. Collards'll be coming in pretty soon." But Lucy insisted that the diet start today.

Lucy put our list and John Martin's chart side by side. "Now for the exercise regimen," she said.

"Exercise regimen!" John Martin scoffed. "Ma's only exercise is lifting a cigarette and your daddy just nixed that."

I rode with Lucy to the market. The interior of the BMW smelled like the head of a new doll. She ran the AC, even though it was cool out. I guess she didn't want to get road dust on the upholstery. We bought enough greens to feed Bugs Bunny for a week—and Mimi for life. John Martin's eyebrows about shot off his face when he saw the register tape, but he paid her back.

For supper Lucy made salad, the one thing she seemed to know how to do in the cooking department. It was right by Mimi's plate when she thumped into the kitchen. "Rabbit food," Mimi huffed. "I'll only eat it with creamy dressing."

"Vinegar and a little olive oil," said Lucy, standing her ground.

Mimi sighed. "Italian rabbit food." She ate a couple of bites and smoked one of her last four cigarettes.

I went up to bed thinking that we were only three cigarettes away from World War III, but I couldn't do a thing about it. So I thought I'd check on Helen, see how she was getting along being fourteen.

I guess being fourteen was keeping her busy. The next time she wrote it was Thanksgiving. Grandpa Bill had shot a turkey. While it cooked they all played in the yard, throwing a Frisbee John Martin had won for being the best reader in his class. *It was a hoot,* she wrote. *Ma ran rite thru the garden to catch it. She mushed 2 squash!!!*

Although she only got the wheelchair a year ago, I had never in my whole life seen Mimi run. But maybe with exercise and Italian rabbit food she'd go back to throwing Frisbees, stomping squash, and running across the grass.

Chapter 19
Whales at the Y

Water aerobics!" Mimi snorted, dropping her sleeve over the patch Lucy had just stuck on her arm. Her four cigarettes were long gone and she was cranky. "I don't even have a swimsuit."

"Then we'll just have to get you one," Lucy said.

"The last time I trotted out like that in public was a class picnic at Wakulla Springs. I was fifteen at the time and curvy. Put me in a swimsuit now and I'll get arrested. I'm a fat old whale and my veins poke out."

"All the Swimming Grannies have weight issues. That's why they take the class. Let's go to the mall and get you a pretty suit," Lucy coaxed. "Girls' night out."

Mimi's eyes twinkled. "Can we get a Cinnabon?"

"As long as it's low fat." Lucy answered.

"Oh." The twinkle died. "I forgot. Anything good is off-limits."

~

We loaded a glum Mimi in the truck and headed for the Tallahassee Mall. There were hardly any suits big enough for Mimi, and she balked when it came time to try them on. "Get me a pack of cigarettes, and I'll try on a couple," she bargained.

Lucy pushed Mimi's chair into the fitting room and hung the swimsuits' plastic hangers on the hook. She closed the curtain, but Mimi brushed it back. "I'm not swimming without Rox."

Lucy pulled it shut again. "The class is for seniors only."

"Seniors plus Rox," said the voice behind the curtain.

"Okay," Lucy said. "I'll talk to them." Since I was part of the bargain, I got a swimsuit too. A black one-piece. "It's so slimming," said Lucy as we stared at my reflection in the mirror. When she left so I could change back, I quit holding my stomach in.

Mimi picked a hot pink suit with a built-in bra big enough for a couple of good-sized melons. "Look at that!" she said, turning sideways. "They stick out farther than my stomach. If I lose a little weight I'll be downright fetching."

Lucy tried to treat us to our new suits, but John Martin paid her back, the last two dollars in quarters. "There's no such thing as a pro bono swimsuit," he said, stuffing the folded bills and coins in her pocket.

~

And that is how I became a Swimming Granny. You'd think it would be awful—and I, for sure, didn't tell anyone at school except Annarose, who was sworn to secrecy. But it was surprisingly okay. The Grannies fussed over me like I was some favorite grandkid. In comparison to them, I looked great. Sure, I was sort of fat, but I was firm-fat. They all sagged and drooped. As Mildred, one of the other Grannies, said, "Gravity is the enemy. You can fight it, but it wins in the end. Always."

Two evenings a week Mimi and I were driven to the Y in town. When Lucy was at the wheel Mimi behaved, but if John Martin was the driver she begged for cigarettes as we passed every gas station, every convenience store. When it came to getting what she wanted out of him, Mimi had had years of practice. First she tried sounding pitiful. "It's one of my only pleasures. What else do I have?" Then she tried bullying. "John Martin, you will pull over right now!" He never pulled over, but he slowed down a couple of times.

Even though she was skinny as spaghetti, Lucy worked out on the machines when she drove us. When it was his turn to drive, John Martin sat in the truck with the door cocked open, one foot propped on the edge of the open window, a book in his hand. Sometimes, when we were circling the pool on our Styrofoam kickboards, I thought about my cousin, studying under the big light in the parking lot.

I worried about him. He was taking on more hours at his construction job to make up for what we'd lost from the Show, and then there were all the special diet things Lucy said Mimi needed. They cost too. Sometimes in the night I heard him downstairs, pacing.

When we were in charge, Mimi and I spread the bills on the kitchen table. I added them up. I always knew exactly how short we were. John Martin did the adding now. But not knowing how bad things were didn't keep me from feeling anxious. And it wasn't just about the bills. School was going better, but no matter what I did I couldn't get anything higher than a C on a math test.

I began to look forward to reading a little of the diary each night. Helen's worries were always the same: boys. Compared to mine they were no big deal. I sometimes wondered how the guys in my class would compare with the diary boys. George Daniel, for instance. Would Helen have written his name in the back of her diary with a heart over the *i*? Could Helen have taken George away from Joelle McBride? Remembering Helen's picture, I was sure that Joelle wouldn't stand a chance. For some reason, knowing that made me feel better.

I reported most of what I read to Annarose. After reading those first few pages she always asked. I told myself that as long as I hadn't finished reading the diary I didn't need to share it with Lucy. Hadn't she said this was my journey? But I knew that was just an excuse. I liked reading it slowly. She'd insist I hurry and get to the difficult part

I knew came at the end. And somehow I felt less like sharing now that Lucy was bossing my family around.

So I dawdled my way through the diary. In slow real-time, we were still a couple of weeks from Thanksgiving—Lucy's target date for Mimi to have lost the first ten pounds—but with the big gaps between entries, Helen was getting ready for Christmas and the Winter Wonderland dance. She wanted to go with someone named Jason who she said was the absolute cutest. I flipped back and checked. Jack had been the absolute cutest too. I guess he got demoted. In Helen's world that meant he had ceased to exist. At least she'd spelled "absolute" right this time.

She wrote:
> *This year I don't need to beg for a new dress. I have money saved from the Leonards. All I need nows a ride into town. Maybe I can go in with Lynda. If anyone ever asks her.*

What made her so sure no one would ask Lynda? **Has a mean streak,** I thought, mentally adding it to my list, which was all I could do. The real list had gotten torn out of my notebook and mushed in the bottom of my pack. I threw it away when my juice box leaked on it.

Chapter 20
Return of the Dragon

Roxanne and Joelle are this year's prize Edison scholars," announced Mr. Franklin. *Roxanne and Joelle.* Our names had never been mentioned in the same breath before. "Roxanne got the only A; Joelle is a close second with an A minus. Good work, ladies."

Joelle looked at me for the first time since the tornado. The shock on her face was extreme. But no more extreme than the shock on mine, I'm sure.

Except in a mother beauty contest Joelle didn't know a thing about, I had never beaten Joelle McBride in anything.

Annarose was so happy for me—ecstatic! That was no surprise, but all the Outbacks seemed to take my A as a personal victory. "Way to go," said Grady Sheehan, pounding my back. "Kick butt, Rox!"

All day I kept sliding the corner of the report out of my notebook so I could see the A and the note from Mr. Franklin: *Thoroughly researched and well-written. Good work, Roxanne!*

I caught Joelle looking at me several times, as if she was trying to figure something out. Once, when she looked at me, I smiled, just to see what would happen, and she smiled back. Amazing.

Maybe there were some subjects where I could be as good as Joelle. I stopped myself right there. It wasn't about being as good as somebody else; it was about doing my own personal best.

Gag! I was beginning to sound like a teacher. The Edison A was going to my head. But it *was* a big A. Maybe a get-back-to-the-Show A. My cousin would know what it meant. He'd tangled with the wizard of Menlo Park when he was in school too.

How would I show the grade off at home? Make a big announcement, or just hang it on the refrigerator like it was no big deal, since I was a good student now? I was leaning toward the casual approach, but as I rode home with John Martin, the A hidden in my notebook seemed to buzz like a trapped fly. I half expected him to turn and stare at the notebook in my lap and ask, what's that?

But there wasn't much conversation.

Him: "How was school?"

Me: "It was okay."

I turned the radio on. He turned it off. He drummed his fingers on the wheel and chewed the insides of his cheeks. Something was wrong. Even the air seemed different, the way it had the day of the tornado. Like Jerome, I caught the smell of trouble.

The smell of trouble turned out to be the smell of cigarette smoke. When we walked in, Lucy was seated at the kitchen table across from Mimi, who was puffing away.

"Oh, Mimi!" I moaned.

"Don't give me that look, Rox. I'm a smoker. You know that."

Lucy's face looked streaky, as if she'd been crying. She turned on my cousin. "Now that you're back, maybe you'd like to answer a few questions. Like why did you do it? Why did you buy her cigarettes? You're an enabler, Johnny!"

John Martin held up his hands. "Hey, it's her body, Luce. She's an adult."

"Not a very responsible one!" Lucy cried.

"Hold it right there, Missy!" Mimi said, stabbing the cigarette in Lucy's direction. "I've been real nice to you. Didn't say a thing when you came barging in, taking over this family."

"This family needed taking over!"

The air in the room shivered, the way water does when an unexpected wind disturbs it. "What are you talking about?" John Martin

153

asked, his voice real quiet. "You're my girlfriend, Lucy, that don't give you the right to boss my family. Them you gotta take as-is." He held up a hand before she could butt in. "If that's a problem, maybe you should shop around, find a guy whose folks come up to your standards."

"How can you let your pride get in the way?" Lucy clenched her fists. "Quitting smoking could save her life! You are *all* so dysfunctional!"

Mimi took a defiant drag on her cigarette. "Thank you, Dr. Oprah."

Lucy turned on her, crying mad. "I don't understand! You were doing so well!"

Mimi patted Lucy's arm with the hand that held the cigarette. "You're a sweet kid, Lucy. You worked your little heart out trying, but this is the way it is. I enjoy my cigarettes, my TV, my food. What else do I have? I don't want to be reformed. I liked my old self fine. I'm tired of eating rabbit food and splashing around pretending to be Esther Williams. No hard feelings, okay?"

"Johnny?" Lucy was even paler than usual when she turned to my cousin. "John Martin?" She was looking for backup, giving him one last chance. "Help me out here."

My cousin crossed his arms. Just like that, it wasn't John Martin and Lucy anymore; it was us against her. Lucy stood up quick. "I need a ride home."

"You aren't staying for supper?" Mimi sounded surprised. "I'm frying pork chops."

"Frying pork chops!" Lucy blinked quickly, and then shook her head. "No! I can't watch you kill yourself. I can't watch your family let you kill yourself. Johnny, are you going to drive me home, or do I go down to the road and stick out my thumb?"

He drove her home. Mimi went ahead and fried her pork chops. She ate two. I pushed mine around the plate and listened for my cousin and Lucy laughing and cutting up as they climbed out of the truck. If she didn't come back with him, I figured he'd be gone a while, working things out with her. I expected him to come home whistling. But he was only gone long enough to make it into town and back. He didn't even answer when Mimi said, "You want a couple of pork chops?"

Except for Mimi's rackety cough, silence settled over the house. Milton hid under the coffee table, which was a tight squeeze. Even the dog felt the change. I had math homework, but I needed John Martin to explain how to do it. He was studying his own books too fiercely to interrupt, so I went up to my room.

I was sitting on my bed doing nothing when Mimi scuffed up the stairs. "They'll get back together, won't they?" I asked.

"I doubt it, Rox." She leaned a rounded shoulder against my door frame. "Lucy Everhart is like a missionary trying to save heathens, only we don't want to be saved. We like ourselves the way we are."

"We could be better. We *were* getting better until you gave up!"

"You think that little hoop-de-rah downstairs was about cigarettes?" Mimi waved a hand. "She comes from a different world. You should see her daddy's office. It's all wood paneling and plush wall-to-wall. I can't even imagine her house. Birds of a feather flock together and we're different kinds of birds, us and Lucy."

"But Lucy likes us!"

"Sure she likes us. That don't mean she wants to *be* us." She shuffled down the hall. "And I, for one, don't want to be her either."

I shouted, "You say that because you don't want to quit smoking!" I fell back on the bed. The water stains on the ceiling hung over me like storm clouds. Maybe it *was* more than the smoking. Lucy's family had money. Everything we owned was patched or glued or held together with wire. Maybe the thrill of riding in the back of an old pickup had worn off.

My cousin said we could work our way up. Lucy was at the top already; it didn't seem as if we'd ever get there. John Martin was smart, hard-working, but at twenty-three, he was still in junior college. Mimi, who wasn't even trying, was busy smoking herself to death. I'd made an A on Edison, a big A, but still... How many As did it take to get somewhere? I thought about digging out my math book and struggling with my homework assignment, but I was tired. Instead of getting the book out, I kicked it—and everything else in my pack—under the bed.

I lay back down, toe throbbing. I missed the Show worse than ever. At the Show we're okay just the way we are. No one tries to improve us. I wondered what Danny Swain was doing. Running around with redheaded Rita, or had he moved on to someone else by now? How was Mr. Finch affording the little extras, like food and medicine? And how about Miss Louise and Jerome, the Gonzalez family? If there was a flock I belonged to, it was the one that settled two days a week under the flimsy tin roofs of the flea market. The fact that I couldn't go there, except in my mind, only made me sadder, so I turned to Helen's diary. Helen was going to the dance with Jason. At least it was distracting, like reading a romance novel.

December 19
Dear Diary,

Jason had this box in his hand when he came up the walk (I peeked thru the curtains). It was an orkid! His hands were kinda shaky when he pinned it on. Ma told him she better not catch him sliding his hand in where it don't belong! I was so embarased I wanted to shrivel up and dye.

We slow danced wrap around all nite. Then he said come on and took me to this little place under the stage he knew from being in plays. We bumped noses a couple of times but then he kissed me! His lips were so so soft. My very first kiss!!! I put the orkid in the World Book to keep 4ever.

—Helen

I raced to the bookcase, knelt, and began pulling out volumes of the encyclopedia. Nothing came out until I shook *J* for Jerusalem. *J* for Jason. Then a papery orchid, as brittle as a dead dragonfly, fell into my lap. I ran a finger over the satin ribbon, thinking Helen wore this when she got kissed for the first time. I wanted to show it to Lucy and ask her about first-kissing. I should've been sharing the diary with her all along. I would when she came back.

If she came back.

I put the orchid back in the *J* volume, and tiptoed down the stairs. John Martin was still at the kitchen table, but he had his head on his arms. I watched him a while to see if he was crying, but it didn't look like he was.

"John Martin?" I said softly. "We are going to see Lucy again, aren't we?"

He lifted his head and rubbed his eyes. "I kind of doubt it. I should've seen it coming, Rox. Me and Lucy are just too different."

"Horse feathers," I said, borrowing an expression from Grandpa Bill. I wanted to demand that he do whatever he had to do to get her back, but he wasn't far from crying. "Hey, guess what?" I blurted out. "I got an A on Edison. The only one in the class."

At first, I could tell he had no idea what I was talking about. Then he sort of smiled. "You beat me, Rox, I got an A minus." When he reached out and gave me a one-armed hug, I could feel his sadness. He had soaked it up like a sponge soaks water.

Chapter 21
Someplace I've Never Seen

W ell?" said John Martin the next night, rattling the keys in his pocket.

Mimi looked up from the bowl of fudge-nut ice cream in her lap. "Well, what?"

"Are you and Rox going to your swim class?"

She set the spoon down and took a drag on her cigarette. "Do we look like we're going to our swim class?"

I lifted my shirt. "I'm ready, see? Why don't we go? We're paid up till the end of the month."

"Nah," said Mimi. "What's the point of splashing around with a bunch of old bags? I'd rather watch the tube."

"Fine," said John Martin. And he slammed out of the house.

I turned on my grandmother. "We could get her to come back if we went swimming and you quit smoking."

She took another puff. "She'd just boss us around."

"I don't care. I miss Lucy!"

I stomped up the stairs, slammed my door, and threw myself on the bed. Part of me wished that Lucy had never busted into our lives, but mostly I needed her to come back. Downstairs Mimi got on a bad coughing jag, so I covered my head with a pillow. When I came up for air the house was quiet. Milton scratched at the door and I let him in. He hogged half the bed, but having that much dog for company made me feel a little better.

But soon I got tired of petting the dog, so I retrieved the diary. "Milt, guess what? Helen just saw her first snow—about ten flakes." I peered over the top of the diary. "I'd like to see snow, wouldn't you? Even if it's only ten flakes." The next entry was about the usual stuff, the Valentine's dance. By then Justin was history, and someone named Mark was the new absolute cutest. *She* showed *him* the place under the stage. *He* showed *her* how to French kiss. She said Mark's tongue tasted like mint. Gross! I didn't *ever* want to know what a guy's tongue tasted like.

The next day at school I had a hard time looking at guys. Their tongues in particular. I'd take one look and my cheeks would get hot—even if the guy was Charles, who would probably never kiss, let alone French, anyone in his life.

I talked it over with Annarose while we ate lunch and we agreed. Lips-closed kissing might be worth trying. But tongue wrestling? Never. Annarose said the fact that my mother was Frenching somebody just proved that she was popular. I wasn't so sure. "Couldn't Frenching lead to, you know…trouble?" Neither one of us knew what we were talking about. Lucy would know if Frenching was okay—if only I could ask her. I couldn't talk to Mimi or John Martin about stuff like kissing, even when things were normal.

And things weren't normal. At home, we were hardly speaking. Every day John Martin seemed grumpier, and he looked terrible, especially when he came home from calculus class.

"Did you see her?" I asked.

"She skipped," he said, sitting down hard on a kitchen chair. "She's bad at calculus. She shouldn't skip."

Mimi ladled globs of cold food onto a plate, shoved it in the microwave, and beeped a few buttons. "Supper will be served in three and a half minutes," she announced around the cigarette in her mouth.

The first night without Lucy, Mimi had fried pork chops. Night two she'd fixed corndogs and double-cheese macaroni. Canned spaghetti and frozen pizza followed on nights three and four.

The microwave beeped. "Here ya go." Mimi plunked a plate of

reheated pizza and instant mashed potatoes smothered in sausage gravy in front of John Martin.

"Getting our cholesterol back up, Ma?" my cousin asked.

Mimi pulled out the silverware drawer and felt around for forks. "Just cooking what I always cook." The forks clanged onto the table. She reached for her Marlboros and lit the next cigarette off the one in her mouth. I guess she was making up for lost time in the smoking department too.

"I'll make myself a salad," I said, but the lettuce was all wilted. The only tomato had a black spot on it. I ate pizza and potatoes, skipped the gravy.

We all jumped when the phone rang. At least two of us were hoping it was Lucy. But when I picked up it was Spice Marie. I passed the phone to Mimi, sure we'd be loading the pickup come Saturday. It seemed like the only fair reward for an A on Edison.

"Nothing definite," said Mimi when she hung up. "The owners hit some kind of a snag with the insurance. There're still no roofs on the sheds, still no opening date." We worked on wreaths anyway, but we didn't talk and joke the way we usually did. John Martin didn't even ask if my homework was done. It wasn't.

I called Annarose, but her mom told me she was doing father-daughter dialogue night at her church. I was in bed by nine-thirty.

～

The only one who seemed to be talking to me was my mother. *School is over,* she wrote. *I'm so glad to be making $$$ again!* She was back at the Leonards', eating Milano cookies and pining for Mark. With school over she hardly ever got to see him, but she used up time and diary space scheming ways to run into him at his daddy's gas station or Wakulla Springs. Then things started happening at the Leonards' that made Mark seem like small potatoes.

July 6
Dear Diary,

Had a pool party for Dr. Leonards students. FSU guys are way different from the boys around here. They talk like teachers. They have hairy chests.

The Leonards kept telling the guys, "This is our baby-sitter, Helen. She's 14." There way of saying hands off!

Roberto flirted with me anyway. He comes from Italy and has the cutest axent! I snuck him my phone number when no one was looking.

—Chow! (that's goodbye in italian) Helen

I had a pretty good idea what Mimi would do if a guy with a cute Italian accent called asking for me. Helen had a good idea what they'd do to her too; she kept rushing to answer the phone. But I don't think he ever called. If he did she never told her diary about it. I looked at the date on the next entry. Helen had skipped more than a month. In the diary time moved fast. I liked that. Since Lucy had left, my life was like a dripping faucet. *Slooooooow.*

August 15
Dear Diary,

Guess what! For my birthday the Leonards are taking me to NEW YORK CITY!!! Their going to a conference and I have to watch the kids, but thats okay. I'm about to get my dream! Goodbye Wakulla County! Hello someplace I've never seen! Lynda sez she likes it here just fine. She's crazy.

—luckiest teen in the world Helen

New York City! My stomach felt strange—excited and scared too. I've never been anywhere. We don't even own a suitcase. I imagined gazing down on the house, the arbor, the garden, the pines. How small would twenty-two acres be from the window of an airplane?

August 22
Dear Diary,

I can't beleive it. I'm in the BIG APPLE on my birthday!!! I thought it wood be like Crawfordville times a hundred with malls and movies thrown in but it is so completely diffrent! Everything is huge and kind of dirty and loud but exiting.

A cab dropped me and the kids at the museum. There were these stuffed animals that looked so real I thought they were alive at first.

We ate lunch in the cafeteria. At the next table there was this lady in an ellegant black dress siping T and nibling a cookie. All day after that I tried to act just like her.

Helen chose a French restaurant for her fifteenth birthday. The waiters sang happy birthday—she said it sounded very sophisticated in French. She had her own room and she sat up half the night watching the street eight stories below: *All I have to do is lift the curtin to see that the city is still wide wide awake.* She was wishing that she could walk around the city by herself, just to see what might happen, when our phone rang downstairs. In a heartbeat I was back from New York, sure it was Lucy. Even if she was mad at John Martin, she could still call me.

"Rox?" John Martin yelled up the stairs. "It's some guy on the phone." Fooled you, I thought, galloping down the steps; it had to be Lucy disguising her voice.

But it *was* a guy—if Charles counts as a guy. "Got a minute to help me with math?" he said. I told him he had to be hard up if he was asking me. John Martin, who was doing homework at the kitchen table, made a gross, disgusting smoochy sound. I dragged the phone in the pantry. I sat between two sacks of potatoes, smelling garden dirt and laughing. Charles didn't really seem to be having trouble with math. In fact he explained the problems to me—using the voice of our math teacher, Mr. Brenner. When I hung up I still didn't have any idea why he called.

"Who was that you were flirting with?" asked John Martin. "Y'all talked for thirty-two minutes."

"Just Charles, and I wasn't flirting." But for some reason I felt all light and goofy.

When I got back to my room the diary lay open on my pillow. Might as well bring Helen home from the Big Apple, I thought, flopping on the bed to read one more entry.

August 24
Dear Diary,

We're on the plane. Emily is asleep with her head in my lap so its kinda hard to write. Today we went to the art museum. The art was okay except the modern stuff. Spud does better with his Crayolas.

But the costumes and armor! There were dresses with pearls all over them and gold thread and a hall full of nights in armor so real its like their about to ride off to save some damsel.

I wish I never had to go home. I'm gonna wanna puke when the plane touches Tallahassee soil.

—Lady Helen

I closed the diary and thought, I'm not anything like my mother. I don't want to leave. I just want to go back to the way things were before the tornado…before Lucy and John Martin broke up. Why couldn't that call have been Lucy? Then I remembered Charles doing his Mr. Brenner impersonation. I had to smile.

Chapter 22
Big Fat Happy Endings

We were waiting for the bell to ring when Miss Llewelyn turned away from the board. Her gaze searched the last row of desks. "Roxanne, could you stay after for five minutes?"

I looked behind me, like she was talking to some other Roxanne. What could she want? I'd turned everything in lately. I hadn't started on the oral history assignment due at the end of next week, but she didn't know that.

The only reason I hadn't started was that I was having trouble finding a story I could tell in class. Everyone else in the class was popping with easy family stories. Joelle would tell one about her mother being beautiful and blond. George would tell about the time him and his daddy went deer hunting and got lost overnight in the Apalachicola National Forest. Everyone in the class had heard it before, but Miss Llewelyn was new. He'd get some more mileage out of it. All their stories had big fat happy endings. I'd probably have to make something up again.

"All good stories are in the details," Miss Llewelyn was saying. "Be sure to involve the senses. What did it smell like?" A few kids giggled. "No, really. There is nothing as vivid as a smell to create a sense of being there."

What being there smelled like in my family was always the same. Being there smelled like cigarette smoke. I wasn't going to put *that* in a story.

The bell rang. "I have to go to math," I said when it was just her and me.

"I'll write you a pass." She perched on the edge of her desk and patted a spot beside her. "Come, sit."

It felt weird to sit on the edge of a teacher's desk with a teacher.

Her stockings whispered as she crossed her legs and leaned toward me. "I never got to apologize to you about that story starter that gave you so much trouble." There were little flecks of gold in her eyes, warm spots I had never seen from the back of the room. "And I wanted to tell you how much I've been enjoying your creative writing. That last assignment about you and your cousin working in the garden as the sun came up was wonderful. I felt like I was right there."

I shrugged.

"No, really. You have such an original way of expressing yourself! Tell me, how is the oral history assignment coming along? Are you comfortable with it?"

"It isn't coming at all," I admitted.

"Oh?" She looked concerned. "Why not?"

The words came out in a rush. "Because stories are these finished things. Like happily ever after, the end. In my family, stories never end. They keep flopping around. You want to shoot them to put them out of their misery, only you can't."

"That's what I mean!" The fingers she put on my arm were cool, calming. "You make such interesting use of language."

Funny compliment. If Miss Llewelyn saw a person bleeding to death she'd probably say, "Isn't that a pretty shade of red?"

"Not all stories tie up neatly, Roxanne. Not all of them have happy endings." Her voice got soft. "It was years after my parents divorced before I even let myself think about it. Writing it in a story helped."

How did it help, I wondered. Seemed like telling the story would only make it go deeper, like carving words in the bark of a tree.

"Your note said you don't know what happened to your mother.

That's a story you need to get someone to tell you." She squeezed my arm and let go. "I may be new, Rox, but I won't make the same mistake twice. If the story you choose is too personal to share with the class, give it to me in writing."

"But it's *oral* history…"

"Don't worry about that. Just collect an authentic story, and tell it from the heart."

〜

"Nice of you to join us, Miss Piermont," said Mr. Brenner when I handed him the pass. Annarose gave me a sympathetic look. Without any idea what had happened, she felt massively sorry for me. The other Outbacks were shooting sympathy arrows my way too. Naturally, they assumed I was in trouble. Who would keep someone after to say, hey, good job? But that was what had happened to me.

It didn't mean I wasn't in trouble. I was.

Miss Llewelyn was expecting something from me.

〜

With no Lucy at the table, Mimi cut corners. The package of paper plates was right on the table. We were down to one fork each. "Who needs knives for meat loaf?" Mimi asked, slapping the forks down in the middle of the table. "It's just more stuff to wash."

After that announcement the only sound was ice clinking in water glasses, and Mimi's cough.

I cleared and washed the forks and glasses so my cousin could do his homework at the table, but all he did was unbuckle the straps on his pack, lift the flap, then drop it again. "I'm going out," he said, and he pushed his chair back, leaving the pack right where it was. The front door slammed. Mimi turned on the TV.

I wanted to ditch my homework too. I wanted to give up on

school but the only thing that might save my life was getting back to the Show. And the only way to get back was to study. I pulled out math and somehow figured it out by myself.

I folded the assignment and put it in the book. It was only eight-thirty, so I called Annarose. When we hung up it was eight-forty—Annarose has a ten-minute phone limit on school nights. It was too early to go to bed, but I didn't want to watch TV with Mimi. I was still mad at her. I got the phone book down and stared at Lucy's number so long I memorized it. I lifted the phone and dialed the first number, thinking I'd hang up before I reached the end. I kept on dialing. Okay. I'd only let it ring once. Someone picked up on the third ring. "The Everhart residence." I slammed the phone down. The Everhart residence? Who answers a phone that way? Mimi had said the Everharts were different from us. Thinking Mimi might be right only made me madder.

I stuck my head in the door. "I'm going up to bed," I said. A haze hung over the living room, and in the middle of it sat my grandmother, puffing like an old dragon.

"Rox, c'mere," the old dragon wheezed. "I want to talk to you." I barely perched on the arm of her chair. "I have a feeling you're put out with me." She patted my knee.

"I am," I said, and moved my knee away.

"Why?" The cigarette on her lip bobbed. "I was just standing up for my rights."

"Couldn't you just go along with Lucy? John Martin needs her, and I need her. You need her too."

Words and smoke billowed out from between her wrinkled lips. "We were fine before Lucy."

"We were okay, but when Lucy was here we were better. We had fun. Remember girls' night out?"

"Remember it? It liked to kill me."

I shook my head. "No. That is *not* what happened. You ate popcorn; you cried and laughed and when you got home you were ready to do it all over again. When Lucy was here, we tried things."

167

Mimi put on her stubborn face. "Lucy can't make me quit smoking."

"No, but *you* could make yourself quit." I didn't even kiss her good night, just went straight to my room. I closed and locked the door.

I dug Helen's diary out of my drawer and held it for a moment. Helen could be annoying and stupid—even mean—but through the diary she had become a friend. I was going to miss her when I finished reading it. Luckily, I still had a ways to go. There would be more dances and dresses and Frenching with guys before I got to my own part of Helen's story.

Thinking about my part of the story, I remembered Miss Llewelyn's expectant smile. She sure had faith in the power of stories. The difference was, she'd had time to tell and retell hers until all the sharp edges had worn off. I didn't even know my story yet.

I opened the diary, but the next handwriting in the book wasn't even Helen's. It was big and round and every letter was carefully printed.

What a stupid, boring diary! Ellie has a bubble brain with mush inside. Her spelling stinks. All she thinks about is boys and more boys. She is a moron.
Signed, Spider-Man

I did some subtracting. Spider-Man must have been around seven or eight at that time. His spelling was perfect, but otherwise he seemed like a normal, annoying boy. John Martin was worrying himself into knots these days; it was nice to know he was a goofy kid once.

A bunch of blank pages followed Spider-Man's note, so many I was afraid there would be almost nothing left to read. But then came a sketch of a dress with sleeves that flared at the bottom. Under it Helen had written, *Mid evil Damsel dress like at the museum.*

She made the dress, altering the sleeves, even though her home ec teacher gave her a bad grade for ignoring the McCall's pattern directions. A junior named Randy was taking her to the holiday dance. Lynda was waiting for someone named J. B. to ask her. Helen was sure he wouldn't. *He's on the basketball team for pete sake!* she wrote.

~

Randy picked Helen up in his daddy's car. No chaperone—big scene. Mimi gave Helen the keep-both-feet-on-the-floor lecture. Mimi and her church friends talked like that. I didn't have any idea what keeping both feet on the floor meant until Annarose clued me in. But Randy knew, and Helen knew he knew. She was mortified. As if that wasn't bad enough, Grandpa Bill jumped in for round two, telling Randy to bring his daughter home by eleven if he didn't want birdshot in his fanny.

Helen swore she'd never speak to either of her parents again.

But they were right. Randy kept saying they should leave the dance and go out to his car, so she dumped him. She rode home with Lynda and J. B.—who *had* asked Lynda to the dance after all.

I felt good about Lynda and J. B. It was as if someone had asked me or Annarose on a date.

Chapter 23
Old Dead Guys

I pestered Mimi all afternoon, begging her to go back to the Y. "We'll see" was the best I could get out of her. But at six-thirty she stood at the top of the stairs in a flowered muumuu, one hot pink swimsuit strap showing. The flaps on her rubber swim cap were folded up. She thumped down the stairs, chin strap swinging. "All right," she said. "Let's go."

"To the Y?" I asked.

"No, to the dentist." She shoved her feet into a pair of old loafers. "Of course the Y! Why give 'em good money for nothing?" My cousin just stood, mouth hanging open.

"Shut your mouth, John Martin," I shouted, grabbing my swimsuit out of the laundry basket. "You're gonna catch flies."

The return of Lucy, step one! I ran up the stairs to change so fast I practically fell over myself.

~

"We missed you two," said Mildred, the Swimming Granny who was losing the war against gravity.

Mimi hugged her kickboard and scissored her legs. "Yeah, well, sometimes I'd just rather watch the tube."

"Who wouldn't?" gasped Mildred, kicking too.

"I swear," said Mimi when she peeled her swim cap off in the truck an hour later. "The things I do for you kids." She gazed at her tragic hair in the little mirror on the visor.

"John Martin, tell Lucy we went to the Y tonight," I said. He grunted. "Is that a yes?" I needed something more definite.

"She sits on the other side of the room from me now."

"Well, you hustle your fanny across that room and tell her. Mimi and I didn't get all waterlogged for nothing."

He watched the white line on the road flicker in the headlights. "Okay, I'll try."

"Try?" I said, remembering the ultimatum he had given me about bringing my grades up. "You *do* it, John Martin. No ifs or buts."

～

My hair was still damp when I dug the diary out of my drawer. There were a few quick entries like *Flunked math test. Got grounded for 2 weeks. Boo hoo!* and *JB asked Linda to go steady. He needs to get his eyes checked!!!* By the next long entry it was summer again. She was back at the Leonards' house. Her sixteenth birthday was coming right up, and she kept hoping they would surprise her with another trip. They bought her the collected works of William Shakespeare instead. *I am such a good actress!!!* she wrote. *I pretended like it was what I always wanted. Plays by some old dead guy.*

The Leonards had another pool party. A student named Andrew Harvest read to her out of *Romeo and Juliet*. The old dead guy—or at least the young guy reading the old dead guy—began to interest her. *Parting is such sweet sorrow!* she wrote. Andrew was one of Dr. Leonard's philosophy students. Big nose, scrawny neck; Andrew wasn't much to look at, but Helen said he had a sexy bedroom voice. She's lucky Mimi never snooped and read her diary. Saying a guy had a "sexy bedroom voice" could get a person in big trouble around here.

She gave Andrew her number, just like she'd done with Roberto. But Andrew called, and he kept on calling. When Mimi and

Grandpa Bill were around, Helen would pretend it was Lynda on the phone. He read her Shakespeare, and someone named Byron.

She walks in beauty like the night, Byron said. Helen thought that everything Andrew read aloud was secretly about her. She wrote, *Andrew lets the old dead guys do his talking.*

She got an A in home ec on the puffy-sleeved Shakespeare shirt she made for him—she'd found the pattern in the costume section of the Butterick catalog. She ironed it, hung it in her closet, and waited for him to find a way to come see her. He didn't have a car.

"I worry about her," I told Annarose the next day when she asked me how things were going in the diary. "She shouldn't be messing with someone old like Andrew." Of course Annarose started worrying too. I had to call her back that evening to give her an update. It was nine-thirty. Kind of late to be calling the Sneeds, and I only had ten minutes. I dialed, then dragged the phone into the pantry and closed the door on the cord. The second her brother passed her the phone I blurted out, "Guess what? Andrew showed up. He stole his roommate's car."

"He *stole* it?"

"Just for the afternoon. He said he'd drive her anywhere in the world as long as he was back on campus by three-thirty. They got as far as Wakulla Springs."

"I'll bet they jumped off the dive tower with their clothes on."

"No, he took her to lunch in the lodge. Not the snack bar, but the *dining room.*" There was a silence as Annarose contemplated eating in the dining room. We'd gotten stuff at the snack bar plenty of times—you can go in there barefoot and drippy from the springs—but we had only peeked into the dining room. From the doorway you could see crystal glasses, cloth napkins, flowers on the tables. I'd worry about my manners if I ate in there. Helen did too. She watched Andrew the whole time to see what he did, afraid of making a mistake. "They ate grilled chicken and asparagus."

"Ugh," said Annarose, "I hate asparagus. Did they swim after?"

"No, it was such a slow, elegant meal they didn't even dip a toe in before Andrew drove her home. She gave him that shirt she made him. He kissed her hand."

Annarose and I couldn't decide if the hand-kiss was romantic or just plain gross. Annarose said it depended on whether or not he got spit on her.

"He called her from the phone in the hall the second he got back to his dorm. He said he wanted to take her to Europe sometime."

"He wanted to *marry* her?"

"He didn't mention getting married. All she wrote about was how they were going to eat snails in Paris. Andrew called them *s-car-go*." No debate about that one. We both knew eating snails was gross.

Annarose's father started making noises in the background. "My dad says it's been ten minutes." More like nine and a half. Mr. Sneed was so strict he even bullied the clock.

"He stole the car again in October," I added quick, before she could hang up. "They rented a canoe. Helen paddled; Andrew played his guitar for her."

"I bet he sang," sighed Annarose. "Okay, Dad, okay. Bye, Rox. See ya tomorrow."

When she got off the bus the next morning, she looked so expectant I felt bad telling her the sad part. "Forget Andrew," I said. "He's a swine. By November he was hardly calling. It was like, 'hey, how are you, gotta go.'"

"How tragic!" said Annarose as we parked ourselves on the bench. Charles was already there, drawing on the back of his math homework.

"Tragic!" parroted Charles.

"Well, it was!" Annarose insisted.

"Charles," I said. "Do you mind? This is private." I turned my back to him. "She begged him to steal the car for the Thanksgiving dance," I whispered to Annarose. "She had this new pink strapless dress she thought would make everything okay with him again."

"Strapless?" said Charles. "It would make everything okay with me."

I shot Charles a dagger-through-the-heart look and went on. "He said he was too old to go to a high school dance. Then he mentioned this girl named Nicole who was with him in a play."

"Uh-oh," said Annarose.

"Oh, it's crying time again, you're going to leave me," Charles sang, then ducked. "Hey, I wish I knew who we were talking about."

Annarose and I huddled closer. "Helen called the dorm like a million times but no matter who answered, Andrew was never there." I tried to keep my voice down. "Finally he picked up the phone himself. He said it wasn't him, but she recognized his voice."

"Ooooh, busted," said Charles.

"He told her that he was sort of dating Nicole," I breathed in Annarose's ear. "But he said that he and Helen could still have a platonic relationship."

"What's platonic?" asked Charles. There wasn't a thing wrong with that boy's ears.

"For your information," I said, turning on Charles, "it's like, spiritual. You know, no kissing or anything. I looked it up."

"I get it," said Charles, stuffing his math assignment back in the book. "Platonic means like, sorry babe, but we're just friends." He tossed the book in his pack and slid an arm through the strap. "Platonic. I'll have to remember that word for future use."

"Like you'll ever get a chance to use it!"

First bell was ringing and we needed to get to homeroom, but Annarose held me back. "Was she crushed?"

"Uh-huh. She cried her eyes out." I could tell that Annarose was feeling sorry for Helen. I guess I felt sorry too. But Andrew was in college; she was in high school. It seemed like they were doomed to break up. Of course Helen blamed Nicole. According to Helen, Nicole had robbed her of hand-kisses and a trip to Paris.

Chapter 24
What If?

John Martin tossed the truck keys up and caught them. "Well?"

"Well, what?" said Mimi, playing dumb.

"You going or not?"

Mimi set her glass of sweet tea down on the table. "Did you tell Lucy about the last time?"

My cousin tossed the keys again and caught them behind his back.

"He didn't, Rox." She took another sip of tea. "Told you it was a waste of time."

I wanted to strangle him. "I thought you were going to march your butt across that room and tell her."

"Wouldn't help," he mumbled. "You're too young to understand this stuff, Rox."

"I understand plenty! You miss her, I miss her, and Milton misses her. Mimi misses her too."

He turned to Mimi. "Ma?"

Mimi concentrated on setting her tea down in the exact same spot as before, matching the bottom of the glass to the water ring on the table. "I was getting used to her."

"Mimi…," I said.

"What? I only want what's best for you kids. Since she left Rox has been moping around. And you, John Martin, you're as sorry as a drowned cat." I stared at her. "Okay, okay! Maybe I miss her a little. Tell her we're doing what she wants, John Martin."

"I dunno, Ma. She's made up her mind."

"What's up with you, anyhow?" She reached up and took his face in her hands. "You plan to be miserable the rest of your life? You want that girl back, you gotta show a little spunk!" She turned her head and looked at him out of one eye, like a bird. "Of course if you're not interested in her no more..."

"Time's wasting if you two are going to get to that class on time," he answered. "I'll start the truck."

"That's the spirit," Mimi called after him. "We'll expect her for Thanksgiving dinner. You tell her that when you see her tomorrow."

~

"Well?" I said the second John Martin walked in from his next calculus class.

"Yes, I told her!" he said.

"And...she's coming for Thanksgiving dinner, right?"

"Nope," he said, opening the fridge. "Doesn't look like it."

"You didn't mess up, did you? What did you say? You told her we went to swim class twice, right?"

"And she said good..." He grabbed a carton of milk, then closed the door with the toe of his boot. "Then she asked if Ma had quit smoking."

Mimi, who was sitting at the table puffing on a cigarette, threw up her hands. "Mercy! Remind her she's dating *you*, not me. And don't she know about compromise? I give a little, she gives a little. Tell her these are my terms. I exercise *and* I smoke. They cancel each other out." She crossed her arms. "That's my final offer," she said, talking around her Marlboro.

Okay, I thought, we're halfway there. Lucy knows we're swimming. All I have to do now is get Mimi to quit smoking.

∾

To get ready for our worst Thanksgiving ever John Martin drove Mimi to the market. She bought a frozen turkey breast, Stovetop Stuffing, frozen creamed corn, brown 'n' serve rolls, and pie. "Nothing green," I said, unpacking the bags.

"So, I'll put a little celery in the stuffing," she answered.

Thanksgiving morning my cousin stayed in bed. "Rise and shine," I called, pounding his door like he did to me every school morning.

"Nope," he said. "I don't feel like it." He was never the type to lie around, but I didn't bug him. Instead I went downstairs to help Mimi, who was getting ready for our so-called family dinner. She opened a can of jelly cranberry sauce and gave it a shake. The sauce slithered into the bowl and stood on its end, quivering, shaped exactly like the can. She didn't even bother to chunk it up, just plopped it on the table like that. "It would be different if your Grandpa Bill was here."

"It would be different if Lucy Everhart was here."

"It sure would," she said. "No stuffing, no creamed corn, and definitely no Mrs. Smith's old-fashioned apple pie."

When everything was cooked and on the table Mimi shouted, "Turkey's ready, John Martin. Stir your stumps." He came down but there was hardly any conversation and no one ate much. Turned out there was no Mrs. Smith's old-fashioned apple pie, even without Lucy. When it came time for dessert, Mimi discovered that she had forgotten to stick the frozen pie in the oven.

I finished up Thanksgiving alone in my room reading the diary. Things weren't going so great for Helen either. She had bragged so much about her FSU boyfriend that she didn't have a date for the holiday dance. She hadn't told anyone at school but Lynda that Andrew was long gone.

December 18

Dear Diary,

I can't beleive I'm sitting home. I helped decorate the gym and everything. The girls were all going on about there dresses and there dates and there this and that. Lynda is going with JB again. Of corse I love her to death but I don't get it. Maybe he sees what a good person she is underneath—that would be a first for a guy. I heard Laura Brandt and some of her crowd saying they didn't think I had any old FSU boyfriend and Lynda stuck right up for me. Described him and everything like she'd actualy met him.

Thanks to Lynda everyone thinks I'm on a date with Andrew. Rite now we're supposably at a play. Hah!!! Some play. It looks just like four walls and sounds like Ma flushing the toylet.

Tears had smeared the ink on *toylet.* I would leave that part out when I told Annarose.

~

The Swimming Grannies all complained that Thanksgiving dinner had gone straight to their hips. "Not ours," said Mimi. "We didn't do anything special." The Grannies all said how smart we were, then Mildred told Mimi that she was definitely looking firmer. Mimi jiggled an arm. "Hon, firm is when you wave your arm and your fat don't wave back at you."

"Well, Rox is certainly slimming down," said Mildred. "A few more pounds and she'll be positively svelte." Complimenting each other on finding the skinny-old-lady-within was something the Swimming Grannies liked to do. It was usually a lie, but it kept their spirits up.

Just in case, when Mimi and I went in the locker room to grab our stuff, I stepped on the scale. I had lost five pounds. "You're beginning to have a waist," Mimi said.

I got all excited. I'd never had a waist before. I wanted to tell Lucy about my new waist so bad, but Lucy had refused Mimi's compromise. She said she wanted her babies to have both grandmothers. "So, now she's talking about having your babies?" Mimi exploded when John Martin told her. "Well, isn't she getting ahead of herself!"

John Martin had turned red when he mentioned Lucy's babies. But he looked hopeful. On John Martin, hope was a really lame expression. He looked the way guys do in those old-time movies just before the pie hits them in the face.

Riding home in the truck I thought, Lucy might see my new waist yet. If she's talking about babies, there's a glimmer of a chance she'll come back.

I washed the chlorine out of my hair, fed Milton, hid Mimi's cigarettes, and finished my homework. When I finally dug out the diary, Helen talked about going to the guidance counselor. Any college plans? the counselor had asked. Helen still wanted to marry a rich guy. Lynda was the one with plans. She and J. B. would go to the same college. All she had to do was talk his parents into it.

I was keeping Annarose up to date on the diary, but she was no help when it came to figuring things out. She thought whatever I thought. I had a few questions I wanted to ask someone older. If there was a chance Lucy was coming back, maybe I should wait and read the last few pages with her. But how would Lucy look at it if I waited—from a psychological standpoint, I mean? She would say I was putting it off because I was scared. And as I got closer to the part of the diary that involved me, I was. But I was curious too—not to mention bored—so after taking my shower and getting ready for bed I opened the book and shined a light on the page.

May 20
Dear Diary,

I can't decide. The Leonards want me to come back but I can get a job at the hardware that pays way better. Lynda was gonna do it so she could hang out with JB but now she has a chance to

work at the daycare and shes crazy about rug rats. She sugested
me to Mr. Tully. I guess I'll take it.

—Helen

Good, I thought. The job at the hardware store will get her away from Dr. Leonard's students. Besides, Helen isn't ever going to be a B-or-better student. She needs to start thinking about finding steady work.

June 3
Dear Diary,
Had my first day today. Mr. Tully showed me a ladder I had to go up to get stock. I wasn't about to go up it and show him my panties—but he said I couldn't go up at all til I read this broshure about ladder safety.
Next he showed me how to run the register and he said he counts the draw each nite and that it had better balance. I told him lissen Mr. Tully I don't steal. And he said Never said you did young lady. And by the way the candy in the jar on the counter is for customers only—not clerks.
Soon as he was gone I helped myself to a fireball.

—Helen

"I felt as if my mother reached out and grabbed me by the arm," I told Annarose, who was seated across the lunch table. We were sitting in our usual spot near the trash cans. "Over the years I bet I've gotten a hundred pounds of candy out of that jar."

Annarose twisted the top off an Oreo. "Me too!" She shoved the Oreo packet across the table, but I ignored it. I had a waist to think about. "How did Helen do at the job?" she asked, dragging the cookie package back to her side of the table.

"Rough at first. You know all the stuff they sell at Tully's: washers, screws, bolts, all sorts of different little things. J. B. helped her with prices. If he wasn't there, she'd get the old guy who wanted to buy the stuff to trot back and read the price off the shelf."

My friend raked the icing off an Oreo with her bottom teeth. "It pays to be pretty," she said.

"Yeah, but she was good at selling. If someone was buying a grill, she'd ask if they wanted charcoal, lighter fluid, hot mitts, or utensils to go with it."

"Add-ons!" Annarose exclaimed. "The same thing you do at the flea market. You're just like her, Rox!"

"Except in the looks department," I said, and made a face. "Her job sounds sort of fun. One night a week Helen and J. B. stay late to do inventory. Lynda's always there, smooching with J. B. behind the fertilizer display. But during the day when Lynda isn't there, Helen and J. B. goof around. He tells her dumb jokes, stuff like that."

Annarose took another cookie and twisted the top thoughtfully. "Sounds like you and Charles."

I glanced over to the next table where Charles was eating with Fred and Grady. He crossed his eyes at me. I crossed mine back. Annarose was right. I could say almost anything to Charles. Charles was just Charles. And J. B. was J. B. "The thing is, Lynda got all jealous when Helen showed her one of J. B.'s stupid notes."

Annarose nodded. "No joke! Helen's too pretty to trust."

I glanced over at Joelle, who was eating at the extreme other edge of the lunchroom solar system—as far as possible from the tray drop-off and garbage cans. She was surrounded by Sara, George, and the rest of her crowd. Ever since the Edison A she had been saying hi to me, which was nice of her since I'd beaten her. If things were different we might even be friends. Maybe sometimes being pretty gets in the way.

~

I found out how "in the way" being pretty could get when I picked up Helen's diary again. J. B. and Helen were restocking shelves, just the two of them; Lynda was at an open house at the daycare. They were having a good old time tossing things back and forth over the tops of the aisles when they had to squeeze by each other delivering merchandise to the same aisle. They looked into each other's eyes, and—oh my gosh, I couldn't believe it—J. B. kissed her! It scared them both so bad they worked on opposite sides of the store till Grandpa Bill picked Helen up.

"That wasn't supposed to happen," I told Milt, who was with me on the bed. It would be like Charles kissing me—a thought that made my stomach sit up quick. With a shock, I remembered what Mrs. Tully—Lynda—had said about my mother wanting things that belonged to other people. Was she talking about her old high school boyfriend, J. B.?

When Lynda stopped by the store after work the next day, Helen hid in the bathroom. If Lynda was anything like Annarose, she would've taken one look at Helen and known about the kiss.

I patted Milt with my foot. "Too bad about that kiss, huh? She really needed J. B. as a friend." Things stayed strange at work, so when the Leonards' new babysitter couldn't make the annual pool party, Helen jumped at the chance to have a little fun on her day off.

August 18
Dear Diary,

Ethan and Emily were so happy to see me I wish I never left the Leonards. The guys from Dr. Leonard's class looked at me like I was really old enuff. Why not? I'm almost 17—plus I wore my yellow 2 piece. I was having fun splashing around when one more car pulled in under the trees. I wanted to dive down and never come up when Andrew climbed out. I waited for the other door to open but he was alone. I consentrated on his bony legs beaky nose and plad shorts. I didn't look at his blue blue eyes. He said hi but not a word passed my lips. At the end of the afternoon he told Dr. Leonard he'd drive me home. Only he didn't drive me home. He took me back to Wakulla Springs.

"Don't trust him," I whispered. But as I read more I could tell that she *wanted* to trust him. "Oh, great! Now he's telling her he loves her, Milt! Why doesn't she wake up and smell the roses? She'd be better off with J. B." But Andrew poured it on thick, telling her that Nicole had been a big mistake, that he'd do anything to prove himself to her. Helen ordered him to jump off the dive tower. They did it together, holding hands, and she was convinced.

"What kind of proof is that?" I asked the dog. "Every kid in Wakulla County has either jumped or been pushed off that tower. All it proves is that Andrew was brave enough to get water up his big nose." I read the last paragraph in the diary entry and got mad all over again. "Oh my gosh, Milt, listen to this: *He bought a cigar in the gift shop and put the band on my finger and said we were engaged!*

They stayed out so late she got grounded, but she didn't care. Andrew was going to come get her. There was a ladder in the shed she told him he could put up to her window when he came the next night, a sixteen-foot extension ladder from Tully's Hardware. All she had to do was sneak down the stairs, but I guess the ladder was more romantic.

I heard my cousin coming up the stairs to go to bed. I switched off the flashlight in case he could see it through the crack under my door. His door clicked shut. I turned the light back on.

Andrew didn't come the next night. She excused him because it was raining. The night after that was clear, and she sat by the window waiting for the sound of a bad muffler and a shadow crossing the moonlit grass. The next day on lunch break she called the dorm from the pay phone in front of Tully's. The person who answered told her she had just missed him. He said Andy had left for Paris the day before for a French language intensive.

I *knew* a little rain hadn't kept him away! It wasn't the first time he'd let her down. But Helen had been so sure he would come for her that she collapsed.

She told Mr. Tully she was sick and asked if J. B. could drive her home immediately. She wouldn't tell J. B. what was wrong, but she was so upset he pulled over. He stroked her hair and put his arms around her. He kissed her again. She kissed back. And this time they kept on kissing.

The diary entry ended there. What about Lynda? I thought. Your supposed best friend?

The next entry was Helen's seventeenth birthday. She had had the usual cake and ice cream with her parents and John Martin. Lynda—who mustn't have had a clue what was going on—gave her stationery. Mr. Tully gave her a pair of pruning shears. J. B. didn't do a thing. He was trying to break up with Lynda, but he hadn't done it yet. That evening Helen was up in her room in her nightgown, brushing her hair out and feeling sorry for herself when something hit her window screen. At first she thought it was a bug. Then it happened again. J. B. hadn't forgotten her birthday after all.

> *I tiptoed over. JB was standing in Ma's hollyhock bed. I told him to get the ladder out of the shed and lean it up. In a minute his face was in the winda. We laffed then shushed each other. We both knew if Pop caught him he'd get a butt full of lead.*

Just like a scene out of a romance novel I could see her picking up the hem of her nightie and stepping onto the sill. I'll bet she took his hand. I could almost feel the way the breeze fluttered her nightgown against her legs as he swung her over to the ladder, although all she said was that she teased him about the ladder safety manual. Didn't it say to never overload a ladder? Then she wrote: *He slung an arm around my waist and said he was tired of being safe. I said I was tired of it too.* By the next sentence they were up on the roof. The tin was still warm when she lay down with him under a blanket of stars.

Perfect, I thought. Romantic. I didn't think anything would happen. J. B. wasn't like Andrew; he was a good guy. So I was confused when the next entry started with the news that her "friend" was late.

184

Friend? Who was she talking about? Lynda? J. B.? Then she wrote, *Its been late before, so it'll probly be OK.*

Oh, I thought, *that friend.* My stomach plummeted. I knew something she didn't. It wasn't going to be okay. I was the living proof.

I realized that I'd read quite a bit. I knew I should close the diary and go to sleep, but I turned the page and kept on reading.

School started again, but she was still working three afternoons a week plus Saturdays. One Saturday morning, she threw up in the manure and mulch aisle. I was embarrassed for her, big time. I threw up on my desk in fourth grade. I stayed home sick for a week, even though I felt okay by the second day. Helen told Mr. Tully she barfed because of the funny-tasting milk she had had on her cereal. He called her a fool for eating it, then sent her to stretch out a minute on the floor in back while he cleaned up.

Lying on the concrete, eyes closed, she suddenly felt deep-down scared. She was pretty sure she was pregnant and she had to talk to someone about it. She tried, but she couldn't tell Lynda. She couldn't tell Mimi. She ended up telling J. B.—the only person who couldn't give her a hard time.

He drove her into Tallahassee to pick up a home pregnancy kit. She said he tried to make a joke about taking a test that started with peeing in a cup, but they were both too scared to laugh. Helen didn't dare take the kit home where Mimi might see it, so she left it in J. B.'s truck.

Helen and J. B. opened the store that Saturday; Mr. Tully was driving his wife to her sister's house in Chiefland. Helen slipped into the lavatory with the kit, then hid it back in the stockroom. They had to wait an hour for the results. But when the hour was up Helen was helping a woman find a jelly bag. Mimi always uses cheesecloth to strain jelly, but the woman wanted to make her jelly just like *Joy of Cooking.* Then she diddled around making Helen track down a certain kind of Ball jar—I've had customers like that myself; they always show up when you have to pee. It was late when Helen and J. B. slid into the back to look at the test.

Mr. Tully returned about that time and found the two of them holding onto each other. Helen was crying. J. B. pushed the test behind a sack of chicken mash with his foot. Mr. Tully didn't see it. All he saw was his whole sales staff in the back, while out front anyone could reach a hand in the cash drawer and help themselves.

Helen tried to defend herself:

> *I said It isn't what you think Mr. Tully, but the old man drove me home without a word. I guess I'm fired. Maybe JB is too—but probly not. Mean as he is Mr. Tully would never fire his own kid—especially one who knows the hardware business inside and out.*
>
> *JB said he'd think of something but what is there to think of? My life is over.*
>
> *—helen*

I went back and read the entry again. And again. If J. B. was Mr. Tully's son then... How could I have been so dumb? Part of my story had been hidden in plain sight: my father. I'd known him all my life. He was the man who gave me candy out of the glass jar by the register every time I came in his store—not one, but two pieces. When I was little, he was the man who put a hand on my head while he talked with Grandpa Bill, the only one who called me Roxy. The Mr. Tully in the diary was old man Tully. A few years ago he had turned the business over to his son. I called the son Mr. Tully. John Martin did too. But thinking about it, I remembered that Grandpa Bill had called him something else. Jay Benjamin—J. B.

I felt as if I'd been turned inside out but I kept on reading. All the slow reading and rationing I'd been doing with the diary suddenly seemed stupid. I'd come to the part that mattered.

"Oh my gosh!" I breathed, after reading the first two lines on the next page. J. B. had said he'd think of something, and boy did he ever. He asked Helen to marry him. "This is the place where you're supposed to swoon into his arms," I told her quietly. But no, Helen was holding out for more than a baby and a hardware store. She wanted to go to Paris and all those other places she'd never seen. Andrew had promised—and then gone without her. J. B. said he would take her wherever she wanted to go someday, but first he had to work and save. "He'll do it," I told her. "He will." I was sure Mr. Tully had never been to Paris, and just as sure that he would have found a way to keep his promise. But Helen didn't want to wait. To her, later was the same as never.

For a while after that she didn't write much. She probably wore loose shirts to school and hoped no one would notice. Like Lucy would say, she was in denial. But it couldn't have been long before people began to whisper.

Lynda was the one who came right out and said it, accusing her of messing around with her boyfriend. Helen admitted that she was pregnant but swore that J. B. wasn't the daddy. Lynda didn't believe her. She warned Helen to stay away from J. B., and then broke off all contact.

Then, all at once it seemed as if everyone knew: her parents, the whole school. I felt bad for her. No one called anymore. No one came to see her except J. B. Once a week, when Lynda taught Wednesday night children's Bible classes, he'd come get Helen and drive her to Tallahassee where nobody knew them. They'd go to a park, or a Burger King, or the Waffle House. He said that his offer to marry her was still good.

"Say yes," I whispered, even though I knew she wasn't going to. "Please, say yes." She wrote *I know I should do it, but I'm waiting for something else.* "What?" I demanded. "A knight on a big old horse?"

In the next diary entry, she stopped going to school. After that she stayed home with Mimi, who tried to talk to her about babies. Helen didn't listen. And all that time I was growing, getting ready for a world that wasn't one bit ready for me.

$\sim$

Annarose opened the chocolate pudding from her lunch bag and licked the lid.

"I got born last night," I told her. "In the diary, I mean."

She quit licking. "Did Helen have a hard time?"

"I guess." My mother had used plenty of exclamation points when she wrote about how long it took and how much it hurt. I didn't get even one for being born. "She hung around for three months. On her eighteenth birthday she snuck into town and caught a Greyhound."

"And that's when she left you?" said Annarose.

"Yup." I handed her my napkin. "You have a chocolate mustache."

"And then...," said Annarose, wiping her upper lip. "Where did she go?"

"She forgot to mention that." I crunched up the foil Mimi had wrapped my sandwich in and tossed it in the trash can. "Better hurry up and finish your pudding. The bell's about to ring."

Looking disappointed, my friend scraped the container clean. "That's all you know?"

"Pretty much." I had only left out the most important detail, the fact that J. B. was Mr. Tully and that Mr. Tully was my dad.

In my mind I saw the path in front of the house. Helen's ride was parked behind the hedge. He sat in an old panel truck with the name of his daddy's hardware store painted on the side, sunrise shining on his glasses.

I thought about it all day. Distracted, I told Miss Llewelyn that "lobster" was an adverb, and I tripped getting into my seat in math. Big laughs both times. I was in no mood for guessing games when my cousin came by to get me after school. "Guess where I got a pick-up job," he said as soon as I climbed into the truck.

I shrugged.

He grinned. "Well, you're just gonna have to ride along and find out." Riding along to a construction job was the last thing I wanted to do—and that was before I found out that riding along included a stop at Tully's Hardware. "Gotta pick up some lumber," said John Martin, turning in.

I couldn't face Mr. Tully. "Let me out here," I told my cousin, pointing to the pay phone outside the store. "I have to call Annarose." I jumped out before he had the chance to remind me I'd just spent the whole day with her.

I dropped my coins in the slot and dialed, my hand shaking. The phone rang twice. "The Everhart residence." The voice that answered was the same one I'd heard before. It was as cool as a handful of pennies.

"May I please speak to Lucy?"

"And who may I say is calling?"

"Rox...I mean Roxanne Piermont."

"One moment," the voice said. The phone was set down gently, and I heard the sound of heels clicking on a wooden floor.

There was a loud clatter. Someone had dropped the phone. "Sis!" yelled Lucy. "Boy, have I missed you!"

"Then why didn't you call?"

"You know why."

"But you should've. You broke up with John Martin, not me. We traded spit, remember?"

"I remember." She sounded embarrassed. "And you're right. Spit is thicker than water..." For a few seconds all I heard was the sound of her breathing on the other end of the line. "So, how are you?"

"Who was that who answered the phone?" I blurted out. "Your servant?"

"That was my mother. We don't have servants, Rox. So...how are you?"

"Rotten. Lousy. I need some psychological advice."

"No way. I gave out enough of that the last time I was with your family. I didn't budge your grandma an inch and I lost the best boyfriend I ever had. I treated you all like some kind of project. But I'm done with that. No more practicing without a license."

"Please, Lucy, you're the only one I can ask." Before she could say no again, I rushed to ask my question. "Let's say I figured out who my father was. And let's say he was someone I know."

"Holy cow, you found your dad!"

"I'm not saying that I did, but *if* I did, what should I do about it?"

"So, this is a what-if question?"

"Right, a what-if."

"Let's see. If you did figure out who your father was, and if he was someone you knew, you'd want to confront him, wouldn't you? Or maybe you wouldn't..."

I had never heard her sound so uncertain. "Just tell me what *you'd* do, Lucy."

"Probably screw up."

"Well, what would Sister Spider advise?"

Lucy laughed. "That old faker? She'd figure out what you wanted to hear and then say it. Wouldn't it be better if you decided what to do yourself?"

As she spoke I was watching my what-if father through the plate glass window of the store. He was helping Mrs. Eustice with a bag of fertilizer. He hefted it up on one shoulder. Turning away so he wouldn't recognize me when he carried the sack to her car, I thought, bet he'd be a great dad. But instead of going up to him I was cringing, trying to hide in plain sight.

I had almost forgotten I was on the phone when Lucy said, "I have a what-if question for you too. What if you had a cousin named John Martin who I stupidly broke up with. Would you say he missed me?"

"Yeah, if I had a cousin named John Martin I'd say he was miserable as a drowned cat without you."

"Really, truly?" She sounded as excited as she did the time I told her he was acting stupid.

"Really, truly. And Lucy, here's another what if. What if you just came back?"

"It's not that easy, Rox. I made a big scene. I stormed out... We both said some things in the truck that would curl your hair. And Johnny can't seem to get past the fact my folks have money. What am I supposed to do about that?"

The loaded truck pulled around from the side of the store. My cousin tapped the horn. "Hey, Rox!" he yelled. "Tell Annarose you'll talk later."

"Gotta go," I said. "Call me, okay?"

"I'll try."

Hanging up, I felt sort of mad. Sure, Lucy and John Martin had to get back together, but did I have to do all the work?

John Martin looked real pleased with himself as we rode along Crawfordville Highway. He grinned when he made the left at Capitol Circle, turning the same way he had every Saturday and Sunday until the tornado. I expected to stare at the open sheds of the flea market as we went by. But the lumber shifted in the truck bed as we hung a right into the lot.

"Whoa! Why are we stopping here?"

"I'm working on the repairs," he said. "Want to help me unload?"

"Help you in a minute." As soon as he'd backed up to the concrete pad I jumped out and walked toward our old spot, two forty-four. As I passed each numbered space I said the name of the regular who was supposed to be there, as if I could bring them back. But the Show wasn't ready for them to come back. While the broken tables had been hauled away, they hadn't been replaced. Our space was nothing but a patch of stained concrete. I put an arm around the post that held the roof up and stared across the dusty parking lot to where Ferry Morgan's cages had always been. Nothing there, nothing at all.

I closed my eyes and imagined chickens talking to each other, and a hundred other sounds: the cough of a pickup starting; the radio on Mack's Boiled Peanuts playing Classic Country; a customer asking, "How much for this grater, hon?" In my mind Mimi was sitting in her chair complaining about the weather. Danny was recommending tires to a woman who was checking him out instead of the tires and Jerome was sending up smoke rings.

I opened my eyes and none of them were there. So many of the things I loved seemed to have scattered: the regulars, Lucy. But I'd find a way to bring them all back. I'd already called Lucy and gotten her to admit she missed John Martin. Even if he didn't admit it, John Martin missed her too. All I had to do was get them to tell each other. I'd hide Mimi's cigarettes so good, she'd forget all about them. And the Show would be rebuilt, starting with my cousin and me unloading the truck. Nothing happens as fast as you want it to, but you have to make a start.

Chapter 25
J. B.

Mimi caught me hiding her smokes. "I should whup you, Rox, making me think I had Al's Heimer's." I wasn't scared; she'd never do it. I was disappointed, though. I had thought she was coming around a little, not making too big a fuss when she couldn't find her pack, but I guess I was wrong. Then, to make matters worse, she said she didn't see any point in paying another month's dues at the Y. "We tried," she said, "but we may as well face the music. Lucy's gone for good."

Something had to happen, but no one was helping me. I went out to the garden where my cousin was tilling between rows, although it was almost pitch dark. "John Martin," I said. "I called Lucy today."

"Ya did what?" he steamed. "Quit messing in my business, Rox."

"I would if you'd take care of it yourself! She misses you. Not that you'll do a thing about it." And I walked away.

I went up to my room, dug the diary out of my drawer one more time, and opened the back cover. The tiny letters inside the heart were proof, I had more family than a cousin and a grandmother.

Do what you think is best, Lucy had said. Staring at my father's initials I decided what that was.

~

The next morning I was waiting when my friend got off the school bus. "Annarose!" I snatched her out of the mob stampeding down the bus steps and steered her toward the bench. "Do you think I could spend the night at your house on Friday?" I whispered.

"Sure. Great! My brother's going on a camping trip this weekend so it'll just be the two of us. Mom can rent some videos. She might even drive us to the mall."

But this wasn't going to be the usual movie/mall sleepover. "There's something we have to do first thing Saturday morning at Tully's Hardware."

She panicked. "Oh my gosh! Is there some project I forgot about?"

"Nothing like that. I'll tell you later." There were too many people around, including Charles, who was headed our way. "It's pretty secret."

"It's something about the diary," she breathed, "isn't it?"

"What diary?" asked Charles, dumping his pack on the bench.

∼

In the summertime, the Sneeds' chickens go up under their double-wide trailer to get out of the sun. Sometimes, even inside, you can hear them underneath, fussing around. But Friday afternoon was cool, and when we got to Annarose's the chickens were in the yard, kicking up dust. Annarose clucked the hens hello as she took the key out from under a flowerpot. Inside the trailer, her dog, Jubilee, let out a sleepy bark.

We kicked off our shoes on the metal steps, then hit the deep blue wall-to-wall shag carpet. Annarose flipped a switch and the tiny chandelier in the dining cove came on. In spite of the occasional chicken sounds, the place felt luxurious. Back when I was into dolls it reminded me of Barbie's Dreamhouse.

Annarose put three slices of Wonder Bread in the toaster—one for each of us and one for Jubilee. She poured glasses of Chek Cola. When she slathered the toast with peanut butter, I asked her not to do mine so heavy. She put Jubilee's outside on the front step beside our shoes. We took our snack to her room and locked the door. Sprawled on her lace bedspread, she read the rest of the diary.

"Well?" I asked, when she looked up from the final page.

"Oh my gosh, Rox. Mr. Tully is your dad!"

~

Mr. Tully opens early for fishermen and guys hitting job sites. It was seven A.M. when I pushed the door open. "Come *on!*" I whispered, reaching back and grabbing Annarose by the arm. "I can't do this alone."

We looked around, both scared, but we didn't see him. The place was pretty empty. An old man in coveralls held a rake in each hand, looking back and forth, comparing. Metal or plastic? Plastic or metal? A woman knelt on the worn wood floor, filling a paper bag with half-price daffodil bulbs.

I had come in here my whole life, tagging after some adult who needed a chain for the toilet or a latch for the screen door. This was the first time I'd ever looked for Mr. Tully, but he was nowhere in sight.

Annarose clutched my arm. "Check the fishing tackle section," she whispered. He wasn't there. I found myself staring at the Milly's Bucktails, Grandpa Bill's favorites. Did I really want to find Mr. Tully and confront him? When I began to hesitate, Annarose nudged me along like the motor on a johnboat. We didn't move fast, but we were moving.

He wasn't in hand tools. Not among the racks of pressure-treated lumber either. As we came around the end of an aisle, Annarose let out a little squeak. "There he is!" Mr. Tully stood on a ladder, arranging stock on a top shelf.

Even standing on the ground Mr. Tully is a tall man. Head disappearing up among the fluorescent lights, he could have been a statue or a monument. But he wasn't heroic like the statue of some Confederate general in front of a courthouse. His boots were as tired as John Martin's. The feet of a plastic horse stuck out of the back pocket of his faded jeans—one of his kids' toys. If Helen had said yes, he would have stuffed my toys in his pockets when I was little.

It was time for me to confront him—he was bound to notice that I was staring. But confronting isn't that easy. How does confronting begin?

Confused, I picked up the first thing off the shelf in front of me, a canning jar. It was a pretty one with little raised apples pressed into the glass. Perfect for flower arrangements, I thought, pretending it was on my table at the Show. Annarose tugged at the pocket of my overalls. When I looked her way she rolled her eyes meaningfully toward my father. I went back to studying the jar in my hand. There were pears in the design. And a bunch of grapes too. Then Mr. Tully began whistling "Over the Rainbow." My skin prickled. He was whistling the same song Lucy and I had sung in our miracle of harmony. It had to mean something. But then the trilling stopped. "Oh, excuse me, ladies." He turned and sat down on the top step of the ladder. "Didn't see you down there. Can I help you find something?"

I saw my face reflected in his glasses, as if I was swimming up from inside him. I remembered all the double candies he'd given me. Mr. Tully had been watching over me for years. My secret father. I wanted to wrap my arms around his shins and hang on.

"Cat got your tongue, Roxy?" he said, smiling. "Whaddya need?"

"A jelly bag." It was the first thing that came into my head.

"They should be right here." He tapped an empty spot on the shelf with one finger. "Sure you couldn't use cheesecloth?"

I shook my head. "Um…no. My grandmother needs a jelly bag. She's doing a recipe from *Joy of Cooking.*"

"Well, I sure wouldn't want to mess up Miss Marilyn's recipe. Let me check in back."

Annarose stopped at the curtain, cowed by the Employees Only sign, but I followed him, still not sure what I was going to say.

When he turned around he looked startled. "You really must need that jelly bag," he said with a laugh. "Just so happens, you're in luck." He held the bag up. "Last one."

"I don't really need one." I felt sorry for him, standing there holding a jelly bag. He didn't seem ready for a father-daughter reunion. But I knew I had to talk to him. The story of my life belonged to me. "I need to ask you some questions about my mother," I said.

"Your mother?"

"Yes sir."

He carefully placed the jelly bag back on the shelf. "Does your grandma know you're asking me about her?"

"No sir, but I think I'm old enough to ask you on my own."

"I guess maybe you are." Then he covered his eyes with one hand. "My God, Ellie." Her name came out like a sigh, as if it was the last thing in him. Then he looked at me again. "What do you want to know?" The corners of his eyes wrinkled in a sad smile and he took a deep breath. "Fire away, Roxy."

If I was older, or if I knew psychology like Lucy, I'd have had a better way to ask my question, but I wasn't and I didn't. Lips trembling, I blurted out, "Are you my father?" When he opened his arms I just assumed...

I fell on him crying and he hugged me tight.

∼

"He's *not?*" said Annarose. "You're kidding!"

We stood on the sidewalk in front of the hardware store, ignoring the ice-cream sandwiches Mr. Tully had given us. "But...but I heard you crying!"

"You know Mr. Tully, he's the soft-heartedest man in the world. But he isn't my father."

"But what about the stuff in the diary?" She lowered her voice to a whisper. "You know…that night on the roof when they didn't look at the stars."

"Nothing happened, Annarose. Nothing big, anyway."

"Then who *is* your father?"

"Helen wouldn't tell him. After I was born Mr. Tully—J. B., I mean—came to visit her a few times."

"You mean he wasn't the one who drove her to the bus either?"

"The last time he came to see her, Mimi told him Helen was gone." Did that mean Mimi or Grandpa Bill had driven her to the bus when she deserted me? I focused on the ice-cream sandwich, which was getting soft inside its wrapper. I tore the end open and took a bite. "He asked me to tell him where she is if I ever find out."

"He still loves her!" Annarose tore the wrapper off her ice cream too, peeling it around and around in one long strip. "And he wants to go to her."

"No, he told me three times how much he loves his wife and kids. He says he just wants to know that she's safe and happy."

I'm not the starry-eyed type like Annarose, but even I saw that there was a little bit of the old J. B. inside Mr. Tully that *did* still love Ellie Piermont.

Annarose dug some of the ice cream out from between the chocolate cookies with her tongue. "Now I guess you'll never know what happened."

"Mr. Tully told me to ask Mimi. He said to tell her she could shoot him if he spoke out of turn, but he thought I had a right to know."

～

The sun was going down when John Martin picked me up. We pulled into our own driveway, and there was Mimi on the porch swing, pushing herself back and forth with the toes of Grandpa Bill's slippers. She looked settled, like an old sofa cushion. "Supper's on the stove," she told John Martin.

"All's I need is a shower and I'll be down." He gave her shoulder a squeeze as he passed and went in the house.

"Come on," she said, and she took a drag on her cigarette. "Have a sit, Rox. Talk to me." She patted the seat beside her.

But I stayed on the steps, facing her, not knowing where to begin. Here I was, confronting someone for the second time in one day and wondering if I *really* had a right to know. "Mimi, what happened to my mother?"

"Tell you sometime."

"Mimi, how about now?" I flopped down on the swing beside her. "I found my mother's diary."

Mimi took another long slow drag. "A diary, huh? I'm surprised. Seems too much like school for her. Where on earth did you find it?"

"In the attic space over the closet in my room."

Mimi leaned back in the swing and crossed her arms. "Well, what did you find out?"

"I found out she was a terrible speller."

Mimi snorted. "I could've told you that much."

"But you *didn't*. You never told me anything, Mimi. Every time I asked you about her, you'd say later."

She shrugged and blew the smoke out her nose. "Why stir things up?"

Grandpa Bill used to say, you can pull a string, but you can't push it. When it came to getting stuff out of Mimi about my mother, I was pushing string. "Mimi, you *have* to tell me. It's too hard not knowing. It's like I'm nobody."

"You're not nobody, Rox. You're my granddaughter." Her jaw snapped shut.

"I *am* your granddaughter. But I have a mom and a dad some-where. I need to know about them too."

She pulled the sides of her robe tighter across her chest, and stared at the sculptures in the yard. "It's hard to tell the trolls from the saints with the sun going down, ain't it?" When I didn't give her an answer she sighed. "So, Helen kept a diary."

"From the time she was twelve until she left."

"Then what is there to tell? You already know everything."

"No, I don't. I don't know who my father is and I don't know where my mother went. I don't know how the story ends."

She picked up my hand and held it. "I always meant to tell you, but it's not a happy story, Rox." Her sad smile was like the last rose on the bush. "When she was little, Helen and me were like you and me. Close. But somewhere along the line things went wrong. Around your age she began to act like she was better than the rest of us. She started wanting to go places, buy pretty things. I think she would've grown out of it if she hadn't gone to work for the Leonards." I nodded to show I knew who the Leonards were, but I was afraid to speak because Mimi was finally talking.

"I knew no good would come out of all that, but your grandpa seemed to think being around professors and college boys would perk her grades up. Fat chance of that. Your father was one of Dr. Leonard's students. The boy's name was Andrew."

I felt a shiver run down my arms. Andrew Harvest… It must've happened the night they jumped off the Wakulla Springs tower together. They stayed out so late Helen got grounded, but she didn't care because he had promised to come back and get her.

Mimi shook her head sadly. "The whole thing about broke your Grandpa's heart."

"She was really in love with him," I said. "I think he tricked her. He said they were engaged." I didn't mention that the ring was a cigar band.

She waved a hand. "Girls who are engaged tell their folks about it. I bet he told her he'd take her somewhere." She blew out in disgust. "She talked all the time about getting away from here, about the places she was going to go, people she was going to meet. What's there to see? The world's the same all over, and folks are just folks."

Mimi was wrong. I'd seen New York, through my mother's eyes, and met the Leonards in the pages of her diary. Fifteen miles away,

Lucy was living a life so different from ours, we could barely dream it. No, there were places and people out there we couldn't imagine if we sat on the porch swing for the rest of our lives. I wouldn't mind seeing them myself. Someday. But I wasn't in any hurry.

Mimi rocked the swing slowly. "Then she went and got pregnant. A big shock but it happens," she said. "Grandpa Bill and I did our best to help her. He hauled out the old crib and painted it yellow. I watched you when Helen didn't feel like it. And then one day, just like that, *poof,* she was gone." There were tears in my grandmother's eyes as she ran her fingers over my arm. "It broke our hearts. It purely broke our hearts. If it hadn't been for you and John Martin I don't know how we would of survived."

"You didn't drive her to the bus?" I asked.

She shook her head. "First we knew she was gone was when we heard you crying in her room. Crying and crying. No, her old buddy, Lynda Smathers, drove her, although I didn't know for sure at the time. When I asked her about it years later she went white as a sheet and made me promise not to tell her husband. That girl was still scared to death of Helen. The only thing she ever had going for her was Jay Benjamin Tully. She don't know how close she came to losing him. Ellie could've walked off with him like that." Mimi snapped her fingers. "I wish she had!"

We leaned against each other, holding each other up, Mimi stroking my arm. "If she had, I'd still have a mother," I said.

She wiped her eyes with her wrist. "And I'd still have a daughter." Then her voice got a little tougher, and I felt less scared. She sounded more like herself. "And if she'd married him, John Martin would get a great discount at Tully's, I'll bet. Well, what can you do?" She squeezed my hand. "Truth be told, she wasn't mother material, Rox. She was dancey as a moonbeam. No way she was going to change all those diapers, wipe your nose, give you a bath every night."

Suddenly I remembered sitting in the deep tub upstairs, Mimi's knees peeking over the edge. She was perched on the toilet with the lid down, grunting as she leaned over to wash my back with a cloth.

"Where did my mother go on the bus?"

Mimi pulled away and took another drag.

"You can tell me, Mimi. Where did my mother go?" I asked again, as my cousin stepped onto the porch rubbing his head with a towel. "Please tell me."

He dropped the towel over his shoulders. "We gotta tell her, Ma."

"You tell her," she said. "I haven't got the heart."

John Martin sat on the porch rail in front of us and hooked his feet through the balusters. "Ellie went to New York first. She called when she'd been there a few days. She had a job as a receptionist, but she must've washed out. When we called they said she'd only worked a few days. About a year later we got a package with a stuffed bear in it postmarked Chicago, no return address, and we knew she didn't want to be found."

Mimi dabbed her eyes with a tissue. "At least she was alive and doing well enough to buy a stuffed bear."

"We got Christmas cards for a couple of years, then nothing. When Lucy started bugging me to track her down, I tried, but came up empty. Lucy wanted to hire a private eye. She even offered to pay for it."

"Bet that didn't sit right," I said.

"You know it didn't. But maybe I should've said yes for you, Rox."

"Why? My mother doesn't want to know about me."

Mimi squeezed my shoulders. "It's her loss," she said. "Her loss."

I didn't know I was crying until John Martin knelt on the porch in front of me. "Aw, Rox, don't cry. You have us. I say, who needs her!"

I saw him through jewels of tears. His hair was spiky from being rubbed dry with the towel. I tried to pat it down. He was crying too. What a time for his head and heart to reconnect! Mimi blew her nose.

"I love you both, so much," I said, my voice squeaking out of my throat. There were only two of them but they surrounded me.

I was slammed into Mimi's bosom, which was like being smothered by a pillow. "And we love you too," she said.

When she let me get a breath, I looked over at my cousin. He was swiping at his eyes with his fingers.

Mimi took one last deep drag and flicked her cigarette over the porch rail. "Jeez, Ma," he said, snuffing loudly. "Can't you just use the ashtray?"

"Nope. And I'll thank you to not go picking that butt up. I want to see that butt lying there the next time I lean over the rail."

"What are you talking about, Ma? It's just a nasty old cigarette butt."

"Yes, but it's a very important butt. I expect you'll want to call Lucy and invite her to come take a look at it."

John Martin seemed mystified.

"That isn't just *any* old cigarette butt. No sir. That's the *last* cigarette butt." She gave me a small smile. "Ya happy now, Rox?"

My cousin sat back on his heels. I wiped my eyes on my sleeve. "You mean I can quit hiding them?" I said.

She lifted a palm. "Hand to the Bible," she said. "Tell Lucy that I surrender. Tell her we'll have her if she'll have us. Call her quick, now, John Martin, before I change my mind. Supper's almost ready. You have five minutes."

He sprang to his feet. "Don't wait supper on me, Ma. I'll reheat a plate when I get home." He was pulling the keys out of the pocket of his jeans as he spoke.

"Bring her back," I said. "We can wait." I wanted all of us at the table. All of us. "Just cut the kissing time short, okay?"

"I'll do my best," he said, vaulting the rail. "Ow!" he yelped.

"What happened?" asked Mimi. He was hopping around on one foot.

"I kicked a gnome." He whipped off a boot. "Feels like I broke a toe."

"You better ice that foot," Mimi said. "Rox, get some ice for your cousin."

"It's just the little toe," he said, and threw the boot in the back of the pickup. "I have nine more!" He drove off, bare foot on the gas pedal. We heard the tires squeal and the engine rev—a broken toe didn't stop him from peeling out of the driveway.

Gradually, the sound of the truck died away. The chains on the swing creaked as Mimi pushed us back and forth.

"Mimi, one more thing. Did she leave a note the day she left?"

"She did." *Creak, creak* went the chains.

"About me?"

"I didn't read it."

"You didn't read it!"

"It wasn't addressed to me. The note was for J. B. Tully, along with a little velvet box."

I breathed, "What was in the box?" Please, I thought, please don't say you didn't open it.

"A gold ring with a heart-shaped setting and the smallest diamond you ever did see."

The same ring I'd seen Mrs. Tully twist on her finger. Tears stung my eyes. That was how close I had come to having a regular family.

But the sadness didn't last. Like a breeze that turns the leaves over, it stirred things up and was gone, everything settling back the way it was. We might not be a greeting card, John Martin, Mimi, and me, but we were family enough for anyone.

Mimi and I sat, resting comfortably against each other. We talked about my night at Annarose's. When I told her about accusing Mr. Tully of being my father she laughed so hard she almost swallowed her teeth. "Poor J. B. Good thing you didn't give him heart failure. He has a wonky ticker." We talked about what I might want for

Christmas, and the fact that with John Martin on the job the Show was bound to reopen soon. "I sure do miss Marie and all the folks," she said. "The church ladies are okay, but they're a little stiff and starchy."

What we didn't talk about was Helen. We'd talk about her later. I'd show Mimi the diary. She'd laugh at some of the stories, and cry about others.

For now we'd said enough. I had found out what I needed to know, but it didn't seem so important anymore. Plus I had a story for my oral history assignment. I was going to tell about Lucy Everhart curing Mimi of all her vices—a family story.

And yes, Miss Llewelyn, I'd tell it from the heart.

Chapter 26
The Show Goes On

Pups-of-the-week!" I shouted.

Only Charles's hand came up from under the counter. A fistful of black-and-white skunkies rattled into the jar.

I scooted the jar of marbles to one side and leaned over the counter. "You hear me, Charles? I said pups-of-the-week."

He rested his chin on the counter. "What kind?"

"Mala-mutts. Come on. Mimi says they're cute."

"Can't." He rolled his eyes toward his dad.

"Mr. Ames," I said, walking right up to him. "Lucy Everhart said to tell you there are laws concerning breaks for underage employees."

"Lucy? You mean that skinny blond your cousin's been running around with?" Mr. Ames turned and spit. "Tell her from me to mind her own business."

"But it's grand reopening day," I said. Tied to every post and table leg, maroon and black balloons batted each other in the light breeze—Marie said the management got a special price because of the colors; everybody else wanted red and green for Christmas. "Please, Mr. Ames...."

Charles watched his father. "Can I?" he asked.

"Oh, all right. Go on," said his dad. "Just get your butt back here in twenty minutes. And don't come back with no mala-mutts."

As we walked along, Charles took a quick karate chop at one of the balloons, making it bounce wildly on its string. He glanced at me. "I was afraid your cousin wasn't going to let you come."

"My grades are getting better. He let me slide a little on math." I took a whack at a balloon myself and it popped with a huge *bang!*

"Heart attacks on the floor!" yelped Miss Louise. Then she gazed at me. "Say, you're getting to be a skinny little thing, Rox. Come back when you're not with Mr. Handsome here and tell me your secret." Mr. Handsome and I both turned red.

Just outside of Miss Louise's range Charles said, "Can I ask you something, Rox?" I wondered why he was asking permission; for Charles it was usually a straight shot from his brain to his mouth. But by then we had reached the puppy table. Whatever he had to ask could wait.

They were cute all right. Big and floppy and yawny. I held one, but Charles just watched. He didn't seem all that interested in the puppies.

Coming back, we had just passed Mr. Finch, coughing among his smoking incense burners, when Charles blurted out, "You want to go to the Christmas dance with me?" We both stopped.

"I don't know how to dance. Do you?"

He stared at the toe of his turned-in foot. "Yeah. I'm Michael Jackson on the dance floor."

Neither of us said a thing for a few seconds, holding our breaths. When we did breathe, it was to laugh. We laughed until we choked.

Us!

Dancing!

"But seriously," he said as he wiped his eyes with a sleeve. "You want to?"

"You're really asking? Really? Even though we can't dance?"

"Yeah, I'm asking." He flicked his hair out of his eyes. "We'll find a dark corner and limp around together. Or maybe we'll just make out." He hid behind his arm as if I might smack him. "Just kidding!"

We had reached his booth. His father was turned away, talking to their neighbor, Miss Rita, who sold silk flowers. Charles snuck a hand into a jar and pulled out a jumbo—the most expensive marble they sold—and put it on my palm. It was heavy and cool, and for a moment I stared at the glass rose at the heart of the marble. Watching the back of his father's head the whole time, Charles closed my fingers over the rose marble. "What do you say?" he whispered.

"As long as you don't expect me to wear a dress…okay."

Charles pumped his good arm and whispered, "Yes!"

I slid the marble into the pocket of my overalls, where it pressed against my thigh as I walked. I was dazed, not sure how I felt. I *really* couldn't dance—but maybe Lucy would teach me. And riding in the cab of the Ames's pickup, squashed between Charles and his father? Scary thought. Maybe John Martin could drive us. If I did decide to wear a dress—and it was a big if—Lucy, Mimi, and I could go shopping for it together. Girls' night out.

Mimi was parked by Mrs. Yu's stool, gabbing and crocheting. I gave my grandma a quick kiss on the top of her head.

"Well," she said. "Whatever was *that* for?"

But I was already halfway to our table. "Lucy, guess what!"

Lucy turned quick. "What, Rox?" She must've bumped something. "Rox" finished with a loud, smashing sound. Danny let out a whoop and started to clap. A bunch of shoppers joined in, carrying on like the kids at school when someone drops a tray in the cafeteria. "Shoot!" Lucy yelled. "Shoot!" She disappeared behind the table.

When I got around back, she was on her knees surrounded by chunks of busted pottery. "Your grandma's going to kill me."

"I doubt it," I said, picking up a shard that said "Okto" on it.

"What broke?" Mimi shouted.

"That German mug with the lid," Lucy shouted back. "I am *so* sorry."

"Not me," Mimi answered. "I been wanting to smash that ugly old Oktoberfest mug myself for the longest time."

Lucy yelled, "Don't worry. I saved you the trouble."

"Save me the trouble of cleaning up while you're at it."

The two of us squatted behind the table and began picking up. I opened my mouth to tell her about Charles but she cut me off. "Hey, look at this." She was holding one of my pipe cleaner spiders. "It must've been inside the mug."

"Lucy," I whispered, not caring about the dumb spider or the ugly mug. "Can I tell you something?"

"What is it, Rox?" She cocked her head. "Wait. Something just happened to you, didn't it? Something good." She studied me a little longer, and then leaned close and whispered, "Charles?"

"Yes!" I whispered back. "He asked me to the holiday dance. What does Sister Spider think of that?" I held out my palm, although I knew she'd just say what she thought I wanted to hear.

Instead she dropped the pipe cleaner spider into my hand. "You tell me," she said. "It's your future."

I meant to look at the lines myself; instead I saw the spider. It had landed on its feet, straddling my lifeline, as if it was about to walk forward. I took a deep breath. "It's good," I decided. "It's excellent."

"You sound pretty sure," Lucy said.

"Of course," I said. "Sister Spider knows all."

About the Author

ADRIAN FOGELIN is the award-winning author of the novels CROSSING JORDAN, ANNA CASEY'S PLACE IN THE WORLD, and MY BROTHER'S HERO.

The idea for SISTER SPIDER KNOWS ALL came from her weekend visits to a local flea market, where she noticed kids bagging vegetables, making change, and working the booths. Weren't they supposed to be hanging out at the mall, playing sports, sleeping late? she wondered.

"I created Rox and Charles," Fogelin said, "to represent all the kids who help their families pay the bills.

"By the way," she added. "The tornado really happened. That's right. I didn't make that up. I just embellished it a little."